On the Observation Car

Stories

by

Wayne Johnson

Other Books by Wayne Johnson

The Snake Game

Deluge (as A. Strong)

Don't Think Twice

Six Crooked Highways

The Devil You Know

White Heat: The Extreme Skiing Life

Live to Ride: The Rumbling, Roaring World of Speed, Escape,
and Adventure on Two Wheels

Baseball Diaries: Confessions of a Cold War Youth

Author's Web Site:
http://www.waynejohnsonauthor.com/

ISBN 978-0-9898604-2-0

As always, for Karen

Contents

Stories published in:

"On the Observation Car"   *Glimmer Train, Best American Short Stories Citation*

"Banana Bread"   *American Way*, in-flight magazine of American Airlines

"Meeting Mr. Donatello"   *Black Warrior Review*

"In Less Than a Breath"   *CutBank* and *TransAtlantic Review*

"Spice Rack"   *American Way*

"Swimming Lessons"   *American Way*

"Stealing Time"   *American Way*

"Eighty Acres"   *Ploughshares* and *Copernicus/James Michener Award*

"Race"   *New Letters*

"Rhubarb"   *Great River Review*

"The Sixth Monkey"   *American Way*

"The Luck at Lord Fletcher's"   *American Way*

"San Marco in Spring"   *Great River Review*

On the Observation Car

Outside the window Nevada flashed by, an enormous desert. I propped my chin on my palm and caught my head when it dropped. Voices tripped and ran, jabbered, intertwined, became one with the clatter of the wheels. My elbow slid across the tabletop, and just when my ear contacted that cool, Formica surface, I heard my father say, "You're cheating."

I blinked, eyes open, awake. We were in the observation car, dome of glass, blue-green tabletop, and over the shadowy swell of my arm, my father, glaring.

"I saw you," he said.

I lifted my head and yawned and looked out the window. In the reflection I could see my sisters, Lisle and Lisa, twins, and Irene, the oldest, across the aisle, watching too.

There was a hush in the car.

"I don't know what you're talking about," the man across the table said.

I affected another yawn and let my forehead bump against the cool glass. The three of them were a sight My father, fifteen years out of the Navy, Ray Bans, flattop, and khaki shirt; the old gent, pencil-thin moustache and turquoise bolo tie; and his wife, heavy, painted-on eyebrows and bright red lipstick.

My father forced his hand down on the table, the cards pattering. "You're cheating," he said. "You heard me."

The wife puffed herself up like a peacock.

"I beg your pardon," she said, and taking pencil-thin's arm, pulled him away from the table and out of the car.

My father held up his hands in a show of mock surprise.

"And she gets mad," he said, turning to me. "What does it mean, Bobby? Can you tell me? What does it all mean?"

I had just turned ten; it was April—Easter Vacation—and we were on the train to San Diego to see my uncle.

I stared out the window. I had no idea what it all meant. Life was rushing at me like that landscape, all rosy buttes, jagged canyons, and wide, desolate spaces. After a time, it was more than I could bear. So I pretended it was Mars outside. We were in a ground transport, destination, City of the Ancients. I had my trusty companion at my side, Rex, with whom I communicated telepathically. Rex was our guide and scout. Only I understood him, and he me.

"Will they have the trillium?" Dr. Turner asked.

Rex thought so. But we would have to barter with the natives for it. I told Dr. Turner as much.

"We'll need you to interpret," Dr. Turner said.

Of course, I told him, I would be honored to do so.

I felt a pressure behind my eyes, a lump in my throat, and in the observation car, someone said, "Full house."

Across the aisle Irene tied her scarf up under her chin and adjusted her sunglasses.

"What've you got that goony look on your face for?" she said.

Lisle and Lisa giggled. I smiled in return. I was not about to tell her. Irene was getting over a case of the measles and was self-conscious about the spots on her face and irritably tired. It was to our—Lisle and Lisa's, and my—advantage, as she couldn't try to play the part of mother, which she'd done since ours had abandoned us, running off to Europe. Two years we'd waited.

She'll be back, my father had said He'd even said it getting on the train:

"As soon as we're out of the house," he said, "there she'll be! Right out of wherever!"

But my sisters and I knew differently. Knew our mother differently, for that matter. Whereas my father thought of her as a *girl with spunk*, we knew her to be *driven*. She was not the sweet-tempered person he thought she was. There was something in her, dying to get out. She'd driven my father's convertible like a madwoman, racing the engine and swerving around corners; she tippled from the bottles in the cupboard and sang crazily to records on the hi-fi, melancholy, boozy show tunes.

"Ah, Pierre!" she said to me one morning. "Let's run away where *no one* can find us!"

My mother wanted romance, intrigue, suspense. My father, a scientist, wanted understanding, structure, balance.

They argued incessantly.

Then, one afternoon, my mother went out for her usual hair appointment, and did not return.

"We've got to stay put," my father said, and so we did.

I hated, at times, staying in the house. I don't mean we didn't leave it at all—we went to class, church on Sundays, the Dairy Queen—but we didn't go to movies, visit relatives, or stay away overnight. My father busied himself with Honeywell projects and bought a new car, a French one, for when my mother came home. He repainted the house, in pastels, and bought antique furniture, some of it very expensive. His tastes, we knew, ran to chrome and glass, but he hired an interior decorator to finish what he'd started, and the house now was elegant, warm, stylish, but not our own.

It was *her* house.

I would like to say her leaving us crushed me terribly.

3

Or that, after her leaving, we drew closer as a family, we regrouped. But nothing of the sort happened. We flew to Paris in April and tried to tempt her home, the miserable lot of us. And after she'd agreed to end the separation, she didn't show at the airport.

For months I thought of nothing but her, fantasized rescues and teary reunions. High in the Alps, a rope over my shoulder, I climbed. Powerful winds blew, crystalline snow cut my face.

"Pierre! Can you see to the top?"

A narrow chute remained to be scaled. Then over, and down the Swiss side. I nodded, waved them on below. My fingertips were frostbitten. The woman, wrapped in a thin, dark coat, slipped and fell again.

"Tie her," I shouted.

Andre got the rope around and under her arms. I began to lift her up the icy face. A crevasse cut at the rope. I resorted to working with my hands alone. The rope cut through my mittens. My hands bled, and just as the rope broke, I pulled her over the edge. Andre, below, gave a shrill whistle.

"You must go on without me!" he shouted.

.

A year went by.

I came to identify more with Andre than Pierre in my imagined rescues, and finally, I fell back on an old, and well-used way of thinking. I had, for as long as I could remember, thought of myself as an orphan of sorts, in the exaggerated way children do: there were people around me, my mother, father, sisters, but they weren't *really* my family. Depending on what I had read, or seen on TV, they were aliens from another planet, Nazis in plain-clothes, or Russian spies. They didn't know what I dreamed of, what I cringed in fear over, and I wasn't about to tell them.

And there were certain ironies in this.

My teachers at school, for example, thought they knew me.

Following a hot afternoon of number-two pencils and dreary, mind-numbing tests, they hung a number around my neck.

4

"You're a bluebird!" my teacher told me, assigning me a seat in the back row, "not an oriole!"

(So what that I'd made stars and what-nots in the margins, played connect-the-dots with those columns of sober circles, and only did the portions of the reading section I took an interest in? And why should I have then, or even now, taken seriously those passages about the mating habits of paper wasps, or burial procedures in Botswana?)

The truth was, I just didn't care.

I'd read a book in which two boys built a rocket ship out of odds and ends. Already I had a number of the necessary parts hidden in our garage for building my own. I wondered what kind of life existed on Jupiter, sketched Jovians as I imagined they must look, given their much greater gravity.

And there were other diversions: I captained submarines, explored caves, circled the world in a balloon.

How could I pay attention in school?

I was smack dab in the middle of a very exciting life.

.

But dreaming myself into another life, I discovered, had certain consequences. On the first day back to school that year, for example, my teacher, Mrs. Hanson, asked, What did you do over the summer? There followed endless, embarrassed, and boring travelogues. The Black Hills. Summer Camp. Uncle Ernie's Farm. Crossed knees, nosepicking, nailbiting.

I told the class I'd foiled an international conspiracy. The President was visiting our cabin. He came down to the lake to fish. Nazis had rigged a bomb under the dock. My friend Paul and I, we'd gotten on our scuba gear, had gone underwater. I could see the bomb there, six sticks of dynamite, a big orange clock wrapped to them with tape. There were sharks. I shot one with my spear gun...

Mrs. Hanson asked me to accompany her out into the hall.

Did I know what happened to little braggarts and liars like myself? she asked.

I told her they got long noses, like Pinocchio. I told her pretty soon I'd look like a woodpecker.

She gripped my neck and we rushed down to the principal's office. He'd make me see sense, she said.

Then I baffled them all by winning the science fair.

.

"Dad," I said.

He was playing solitaire, slapping the cards down smartly. "What, Bobby?" he said.

The train jolted over a rough section of track.

"How much further is it?"

"Days."

"How many days?"

"Two days. Why don't you go over and play cards with Lisle and Lisa and Irene? Or read your book?"

"I'm tired of sitting."

"Well, so am I," he said, glancing up at me. "So what?"

.

I imagined sticking pins in his neck.

I knocked his coffee in his lap. Tossed his cards out the window and yanked on his ears. Poked him in the chest with my finger, the way he did me.

That's so what!

I brooded beside him. After a time he wrapped his arm around me and squeezed.

"You okay?" he asked.

"Great," I said.

.

We were going to see my uncle Carl. I loved Carl.

I was his hiking buddy before they'd moved, Carl and his family. At least once a week, Carl, my father, and I had taken the stairs down the River Road to hike along the Mississippi. There were caves in the sandstone, with people's names and dates scratched deep into the walls. The river washed up debris that was fascinating to me: Melmac plates,

6

soda bottles, bowling pins, car seats—you name it. Each time was different.

"What do you got there, ol' buddy?" Carl would tease.

The beaches smelled fishy and had sturdy, semiaquatic brush growing on them. My father had his eye on what I picked up.

"Bobby," he'd say, "put that down."

And Carl would reply, "Oh, he's all right."

Sometimes, when my father got that look, all angles, his mouth set and angry, Carl would scoop me into his arms—he was a big man—and spin me around.

"Oh, you're my best buddy!" he'd say, and rub his knuckles over my head.

I was crazy about him. He had an expansive laugh, smoked cigars of an especially smelly variety, wore his clothing loose, and at dinner, drank "highballs" and enjoyed them, drank them right down, rattling the ice in his glass.

"Ahhhhh!" he said. "Now *that's* a drink!"

Somehow, Carl owned the world.

It didn't matter that his car was dented and old, that his garage was a mess. The Bay of Pigs business, as he called it, did not scare him.

It'll work out, he said.

.

After Carl left, my father and I hiked. But it was not the same thing at all. Those afternoons I dreaded. My father, as my grandmother put it, walked like a house afire. He got to thinking—which was most of the time—and then he wasn't there. He charged along at a furious pace, arms windmilling, and I couldn't keep up, and for the life of me, I couldn't force myself to shout, "Slow down!" or "Wait!" There was no point to it. Because, though I minded him tearing away from me, I hated even more his angry silences. He was always worked up about something, and he took it out on me. I was the only boy. Somehow that made me special. I was *responsible*, he said. He was saying that to me from the time I could walk.

.

Carl, on the other hand—

"Let's go have an ice cream," he'd say.

"You're getting a little big around the middle, aren't you?" my father would counter.

"That's my happy roll," Carl would say, and sweep me off the sidewalk. "Tallest man in the world! What does it look like from up there, Chief?"

"High!"

"Airplanes getting in your hair?"

.

I lived, for a time, in his company. The world was my oyster, he said. And with Carl, the world was a friendly place, something you might want, after all. He drove with the windows down in November—"Smell those leaves!"—ate enormous pecan rolls for breakfast and washed them down with cups of scalding, black coffee. "Boy, that's good," he'd say.

He golfed until it snowed.

"Can't see the goddamned ball," my father would say.

But we trudged along anyway, the snow ankle deep in places.

"I'll just throw another ball down," Carl would say. "How many strokes was that? Four or five?"

"Eight," my father would correct, a certain irritation in his voice.

And always, I was there, with them, with Carl.

With Carl I was not too short, too weak, too small, not boy enough. With Carl my grades were not important, nor were my teachers and classmates.

"What are you reading?" Carl would ask. "So how are you going to build this spaceship?"

Crowded into a tiny booth, a malt mixer roaring away in the back, he listened, pressed me for details, while my father, his head turning one direction and then the other, watched people, women especially.

.

On the observation car I watched him at it: rubbernecking, I think people called it.

"See that lady over there, by the coffee urn?" he asked.

I craned my head around to look. The car was filled to capacity. I remember feeling a certain nervous confusion. How was I supposed to know who he meant? And why was he asking me?

"Over there," he said, "in the corner."

She was reading and drinking a cup of coffee.

"What about her?" I said.

I felt uncomfortable looking directly at her—so I watched her in reflection: auburn hair, swoopy eyes, and full mouth. Looking at her sent prickles up my back. My father smiled and motioned for her to come sit with us. The woman set her book down and slid out from her table with a certain drowsy, but menacing agility.

"I gotta go," I said, and hurried off in the opposite direction, out of the car, toward the diner.

I had a malted milk. And a hamburger. And fries.

The waiter was a quiet-speaking black man and teased me about my appetite.

"Would the gentleman like another plate of fries?" he asked.

I said I would.

In a sudden vicious spree, I was spending all my hard-earned lawn-mowing money. I tried not to think about my father. I ordered another malted milk. I made tents out of napkins, staged Civil War battles.

You're needed at the front! Captain Pearson shouted, guns firing from all sides.

The waiter stopped by again. The diner was getting busy.

"Is the Mr. finished?" he asked.

I knew he was politely asking me to leave. I told him no and got another hamburger.

.

Somewhere between the third and the fourth hamburger I got motion-sickness. The car rattled and bolted. My head swam. I paid the waiter, left what I thought was a sufficient tip, and calmly carried myself out of the car, then ran, looking for what-I-didn't-know.

.

When I could breathe again, I shook my head.

The tracks stretched out and away to the left. I'd hung my chin over the restroom window and made a mess of it. Where my eyes watered my face stung with cold. I breathed deeply, and was again in the throes of it. Someone banged on the door behind me. I gripped the windowsill.

"Is someone in there?"

After a time they went away. I waited until I could take a deep breath without feeling my stomach rise. I looked in the mirror. The light made my face look blue. My hair was thrown back from my forehead, my eyes bloodshot, my shirt rumpled. And I smelled. I washed my mouth out and combed my hair. Or tried to.

It was impossible, and in the end, I wetted the whole mess and raked it flat.

.

"I'd like you to meet my son, Bobby," my father said. "Bobby, this is Virginia."

I didn't want to, but I put my hand out.

"Hello," she said.

.

I wanted her to be awful. I wanted to hate her. I wanted her to say something that would pit me against her, once and for all.

(My mother was out there, after all.)

My father bent over the table, explaining something. It was his sales spiel; he'd sold dictionaries in the South during the late thirties and could really ramble. The car tripped along with his voice. It had a certain hypnotic effect. I was trying not to stare at Virginia. She was wearing a violet sweater, one especially soft and fuzzy.

"Excuse me," she said.

She leaned over the table, put her hand on my forehead. Her hand was smooth and warm. It made me drowsy. She worried the corner of her lower lip between her teeth. She brushed the hair back off my forehead, and let her hand rest on my cheek.

She looked right in my eyes, nodded, then turned to my father.

"I think he's a little sick," she said. "You're a little sick and worn out, aren't you?" she said to me, and I wanted to crawl right up into her lap.

In our sleeper compartment I lay awake, the train rattling, surging along. I identified variations in the sound—the *clack-slap* of switches outside town—and imagined teenaged boys rolling a log in front of the train, the train derailing.

"Get on the end there, Huff," I said.

We were all liquored up and having a good time.

"Stupid sons of bitches'll never know what hit 'em," Huff said. The log was sticky, covered with resinous creosote. I had it all over my hands.

"They're gonna catch us if we can't get this off," I said.

"Fuck 'em," Huff said.

I gripped the bunk and braced myself for the collision.

I thought about Virginia. She had that nearly translucent, freckled skin auburn-haired women have. And her irises were reddish brown. One eye was higher than the other, not really noticeably so, but it gave her a certain look, one I twisted into grotesque proportions in the dark.

I hated her. I really did.

I hated everything about her. I hated her deep, reedy voice. I hated the way she held her hands, twining her slim fingers into a warm knot. I hated her perfume—a faint, dusty smell. I hated the way she walked, hated the sad, cloying way she smiled.

"A year," she'd said. "He wanted it."

In the dark, I listened to my sisters, Lisle and Lisa and Irene, breathing. I wished I could sleep. I wanted to say something terrible to Virginia, to make her go away. I tried to think what. The problem was I didn't want to be embarrassed doing it. I knew almost nothing about her. What could I say? I was only ten, it was beyond me. All I knew was she was lovely, lonely, had a voice that sent shivers up my back, and I hated her.

And then it occurred to me what I should do:

"Irene," I said. I was in the top, smaller bunk. "Irene," I said, reaching down, shaking her awake.

Sharp-tongued, clever Irene.

We ate an endless breakfast in the dining car.

I looked for Virginia. She was nowhere in sight. The old card sharks took a table to our left, and my father sat upright and indignant through the whole meal, and so did the man and his wife.

"Cheaters," my father said, when we finally stood to go.

"Nincompoop," the woman said, as soon as our backs were turned.

"What?" my father said.

But all that came from the car was the sound of silverware on china, the clatter of pots and pans in the kitchen, and the low mutter of conversation.

It was our last day on the train.

I sat on the north side of the observation car, intrigued by the cactus, the eroded gullies, the now almost aquamarine stretch of sky to the west. Everything was rose, ocher, and this peculiar, saturated blue.

I imagined meeting Carl at the train station. My father had called a few stops back. Carl was to meet us around six. I pictured him standing to one side of the tracks, eating something, a doughnut, a Danish, a creme-filled something, a smile on his face. Imagining it, I felt a kind of homecoming.

"Tide pools," Carl had said on the phone. "You'll love 'em. Full of all kinds of things. Anemones, starfish, coral, sea cucumbers, brine shimp."

"What's a sea cucumber?" I asked.

"It's an animal, for one."

"How can a cucumber be an animal?" I wanted to know.

"You'll see," Carl reassured me.

Irene took the phone. I resented her doing it. I wanted Carl all to myself. "Disneyland?" she tittered.

Then Lisle and Lisa.

And all the while, I guarded what Carl had said to me as though it were the most precious thing in the world.

"You're my best buddy, Bobby," he'd said. "You can count on it."

Each mile was a mile closer. The ocher expanses became grass, grass trees, then homes. It was lunchtime. My father went off for sandwiches and returned with four.

"Gotta go back. Huge line. Don't wait," he said, then strode from the car, a peculiar spring in his step.

My sisters and I looked at each other.

"Just shut up and eat," Irene said.

I was starving and ripped the cellophane off my sandwich. I was embarrassed, yet relieved, that Virginia hadn't made an appearance at our table as I'd claimed she would.

"Stop eating like a pig," Irene said.

Lisle bent over her plate, crying, and Lisa started in. Irene glared across the table.

"So this is your idea of a big joke, huh?" she said. "I'll get you back, Bobby."

I blinked. My heart beat a little harder.

"I made it all up!" I blurted, and ran from the car.

.

My father was not in the diner. And he was not in his sleeper, or in ours. I felt a certain relief, but then an even greater shock. I strode purposefully up and down the cars, the train swaying and rattling along. The trees outside flashed by, almost as if torn back from behind. Finally, running into a porter wearing a gold cap and red jacket, I composed myself.

My father had sent me down the train to deliver an invitation to a certain lady, I said. I'd forgotten her compartment number and my father was going to give me hell for it.

"Her name's Virginia," I said, my voice quavering. "At least I think it's Virginia."

13

And at the second mention of her name I lost it.

And that, I think, was what convinced the Porter.

.

At Virginia's door I stood looking out the window.

Streets spun by like spokes in a wheel.

They're not in there, I told myself. But I couldn't bring myself to knock.

There was a railing, and people squeezed by with their luggage. I went to the end of the car and waited in the warm vestibule. I stood on my toes trying to see through the window into the car. It was almost impossible to keep my balance. There were gaps in the floor, where the cars came together. The cars rocked and bucked. The vestibule smelled of grease and diesel fuel. I held a long metal arm, felt as if I were on the back of some enormous, bucking and pitching animal. I was sweating. It got cold in there, and using that as an excuse, I went back out front of Virginia's door.

Did I hear something? A bumping sound? Or was it the train?

I put my hand in my pocket, tried to keep my mind on the trees out the window. I had never seen palm trees. And just like that, I spun around and knocked.

Rap-rap-rap.

Was that someone crying?

"Who is it?" Virginia said, over the rattle and clatter. "Who's there?"

I bolted, ran the length of the car. And throwing back the door of the vestibule, I knocked an elderly couple down, the wife's suitcase popping open, the contents, clothes and bric-a-brac, flying every which way.

I tried to say I was sorry, then recognized them: the cheaters.

"You should be ashamed of yourself, Young Man," the woman said.

Then they were gone, suitcase and all.

I stood on my toes and peered through the vestibule window. Two men were walking the length of the car, one toward me, the other turning the corner to the next ahead, hat cocked rakishly to his left, his arms swinging at his sides. Had my father been wearing a hat? Virginia's door opened and she stepped out, touched her hair.

She smiled to herself. Beautiful.

I hated her.

Another compartment door opened. More men. Two in gray suits. Lunch over, the car was crawling with people. I stared out the vestibule window, everything a blur.

.

I pressed my face against the canopy glass. The glass was cool, tinged with orange. The sun was setting. City lights blinked on as far as I could see—whole constellations of them. I turned in my seat and spun my book on the tabletop.

The car was nearly empty now but for a young couple kissing and whispering in back and the card sharks in the booth furthest forward. They were both wearing sunglasses and busied themselves with their luggage. My father, across the table, was reading *Scientific American*. Irene was bullying Lisle and Lisa through another card game behind us.

"Liar," she whispered fiercely and poked me in the back.

"Why don't you read there, buddy?" my father said.

I shrugged, and gave the book another spin. *Lodestar, Rocketship to Mars*. I couldn't bear to read so much as a word of it now. I stared out the window, the car in reflection riding ghostly over the California night.

I imagined the canopy of the observation car to be that of a Supermarine Spitfire. I tailed Heinkel bombers and Messerschmidt fighters. Ra-tat-tat-tat-tat. The curves in the track simulated banks and dives. Commander Thruxton, R.A.F. ace extraordinaire, shot down one plane after another.

But it was all wrong somehow.

So I imagined myself Wolfgang Gottlieb, in a burning bomber instead.

"Get out!" I shouted.

My crew jumped, bright parachute bursts in the moonlight. Smoke filled the cockpit. I desperately searched the ground for a place to land.

Spitfires came from every direction. Bullets tore at the fuselage, tail, wings. There was a flash of light. Glass shattering in the cockpit—

"What are you thinking so hard about?" my father asked.

I studied the hat on the seat beside him and remembered those swinging arms.

The car jolted.

Now, outside the station, I could see shining rails, crazed, running all directions. They criss-crossed, curved back on themselves, shot off to the left and right. Big, broadsided station boxes, green and red and blue, loomed larger, then vanished behind us.

I studied my father's face.

"How long is it now?" I said.

My father set his magazine on the table and glanced at his watch.

"Minutes. You excited?"

I nodded. The intoxicating light of San Diego grew stronger, flashed in the observation car canopy. I thought about Carl, and for a time there, the world swelled, an enormous fortune cookie—Carl had called it that one afternoon. And then the train slowed.

The station roof slid back over the observation car. The *tadada, tadada, tadada* of the wheels became an ambling *clack, clack-clack*. The train eased into the station, brakes hissing. The station, all concrete and steel and bright, orangish light, seemed preternaturally real.

The train gave one last, tired surge and came to a stop.

"We're here!" my father said, and Irene ushered Lisle and Lisa out.

I followed behind my father. The steps off the observation car were especially long, and the porter helped people down.

"You take care now," he said, and winked at me.

People were standing in circles, blinking in the orange light. Railmen in blue uniforms threw luggage onto huge, steel-wheeled carts and rolled them away, passengers following. The station smelled of diesel exhaust, hot oil, electricity, and perfume, fusty body odor and cologne.

The two lovers stepped around and in front of me. I could barely see over their shoulders. My father, in his usual way, strode out across the platform, Irene and the twins behind him.

My heart gave a big kick—there was Carl, open coat flapping at his sides, running. He seemed older than I remembered, tired. But he smiled, and something like heat made me smile in return. My father put out his hand and Carl took it, pulled him into his arms and hugged him, slapping him on the back.

Carl let go and a cluster of passengers pushed by. He stooped, hands on his hips.

"So," he said.

He looked from Lisle to Lisa to Irene, then shook my father's hand again.

I couldn't move.

"So," Carl said again. "Are we all here?"

Something as big as an apple caught in my throat. I could have gone around to the side but something compelled me to stand there behind that couple, testing him.

Carl kissed each of my sisters.

My father turned his head—for a second I thought he was looking for me. There was a certain secretive set to his face. The card sharks strode by, pencil-thin bringing his cane down hard, the woman with her nose in the air.

"Nincompoop," she said.

And then came Virginia, a porter carrying her bag, navy blue coat, her auburn hair like coals down and over her shoulders. She gave the slightest nod and my father tipped his hat.

"Somebody we met on the observation car," he said.

Irene frowned. Carl winked at my father and clapped his hands together.

"So, should we head out to the car?" he said, and I felt my legs buckle under me.

.

A moment later, the situation was righted. Carl squeezed me in a bear hug and told me how glad he was to see me. I stiffened and did not hug him in return.

"Okay," he said, and we went out into the parking lot.

There, in my childish way, I enjoyed seeing him stumble with the luggage and fuss consciously over the seating arrangements.

"How's my boy?" he said, when we'd all gotten in.

"Fine," I said. I knew the score.

But of course, there were things I didn't know then, and would not know for years, decades even.

I didn't know that Carl's son was having terrible difficulties with alcohol, ones that would eventually kill him. Or that his daughter's husband was a wife-beater and sent her home with black eyes.

I didn't know that Carl couldn't afford to pay the taxes on his house, or that my father was footing a portion of the bill.

I didn't know how tired Carl was, or that his daughter's husband had hit him, in his garage, before he came to get us.

Or that he cried, talking to my father that night.

At his house, up high and overlooking the ocean, we got out of the car. The porch light was on. Edna, my aunt, opened the door and welcomed us in. My father, laughing, and Irene and the twins, went through the door. Carl and I stood out in the dark. I could tell he wanted to say something to me.

"Bobby," he said.

He got down on one knee and looked in my eyes. He was a big man.

"You're still my best buddy," he said.

What could I say?

The air was full of new smells: floral scents, the ocean—rich, damp, complex—and eucalyptus. Heat came up off the concrete drive. The surf roared blocks away.

It was a new and terrifying world.

"Give me a big bear hug," Carl said, and threw his arms around me.

18

I stood there, my arms at my sides.

"Come on, Bobby."

I shrugged and let my head fall back. The stars seemed infinitely small and distant, swallowed up in all that blackness.

"We're gonna build that spaceship, aren't we?"

Carl gave me a little shake.

I kicked at the drive. There was a terrible knot in my throat; I couldn't swallow.

"That's stupid," I heard myself say. "Anybody knows you can't make a spaceship out of old tins cans and junk."

1

Little Matters of Consequence

Banana Bread

It was the day school was to start, and the boy and his mother were having a difficult time of it: she, for the significant thing his leaving was; the boy, for the loss of freedom school represented. In the kitchen he played with his cereal and did not eat well. If I'm sick, he thought, she won't send me. The boy's mother was unusually quiet. She sat across the table, smiling. She had a thermometer in her pocket and was prepared to circumvent this latest of ploys—fever. All morning he'd tested her.

The canary sang in its cage.

"Shut up, Chirry," the boy said.

"Toby," said his mother.

The boy went back to his cereal. Outside the milk truck stopped, and Larry, their milkman, tromped across the yard and shouted through the open windows.

"Larry here! Beautiful day, isn't it?"

Toby's mother opened the door and took the bottles.

"Thank you," she said. She tipped him, and came back into the kitchen. She put the bottles in the refrigerator. Toby's sister, two years younger, pulled her blanket up the hallway, her thumb in her mouth.

"Mom doesn't want you to do that," Toby said, and Anne took her thumb out of her mouth.

"Why not?"

"Because."

"Because what?"

"Because it'll make your thumb get longer."

Anne examined her thumb, then held it solemnly against her stomach.

"Will not."

"Will so."

"Toby's fibbing again," Anne said.

The children's mother closed the refrigerator door. Her eyes were red.

"Wash up, Toby," she said. "We're going in a few minutes.

The bus stop was only blocks away, but the walk seemed to take forever. Anne skipped and hummed; Toby had a sudden impulse to hit her, but didn't. His mother reached for his hand and he pulled it away. He slapped his Buster Browns down, slap, slap, slap. Ran to the Vegans' lawn and fell onto his back. The sky above was blue, bright blue, the Vegans' big oak cutting into it the most delicious red.

A dog barked in a far-off yard. He could hear it throwing itself against the fence.

"Toby!" his mother called.

In the middle of the road, the bus stop and other children in sight, she spun him roughly around and adjusted his clothes. Her fingers pinched, and he felt something hot at the back of his throat. Anne smiled off to the side, and he wanted to hit her again.

"All right," Toby's mother said, and gave him a brief, fierce hug, and pushed him in the direction of the boys and girls down the block.

He could feel her eyes on his back. He tossed his shoulders, as if trying to throw off the imprint of her hands. He kicked and scuffed up the hill, slower, and then, from the opposite direction, the big, orange-yellow bus rumbled, grew larger.

Toby stopped and turned.

Anne waved. He waved back. His mother stood with her arms over her chest, looking away. Then he waved again, and climbed the last of the hill, and got into line with the others.

She watched the bus ease back, heard the motor rev, and then the bus lurched forward, bright in the sun, orange and black and yellow. She tried to make out Toby's face in one of the windows, the bus turning the corner. She could make out each and every seat, the neighbors' children, smiling and waving.

And then the bus was gone.

She looked to both sides of the bus stop, blue mailbox, a large pine, one pastel split-level after another, a vague uneasiness settling in her.

"Is he coming back?" Anne asked.

The girl's mother bent to tie her shoelace. It had come undone.

"Yes," she said, and they turned toward the house.

Toby waited until his mother and Anne had gotten to the end of the block, crossed the lawn, and gone into the house, then breathed easier. It was quiet and dark under the pine tree. He had seen the tree weeks earlier, but only at the last second had he thought to scoot under its branches. Now two women chatted where the bus had been.

"Well, that's the last," the shorter of the two said.

The taller woman, in turquoise slacks, held her hand over her eyes. The dog was barking again.

"I'd better go back," the shorter said.

"I'll wait," said the other.

They walked in opposite directions. Birds darted by, calling shrilly. There was more talking up the block, and uneasy laughter. But it was of no importance now, and Toby slid out on his stomach, dusted himself off, then quickly went across the street and into the woods.

Alone, and in the woods, he allowed himself luxuries he was usually denied: Indians didn't wear shoes, so he took his off. He climbed a large boxelder and explored the cattails and water further in. At one time there had been a lake, but now all that remained was a marsh, and he waded out into the muck until it covered his knees. Ducks clucked and swam in circles in the shallow water. Toby, when he got tired of watching them, threw stones, as he had been taught not to. The ducks eyed him with a kind of sullen disapproval, it seemed, moving beyond the range of his stones, and he quit that, then turned back to the path and trees.

Midway, he stopped, wondering what to do.

His freedom, now that it had stretched into the afternoon, had become a little troublesome. He was hungry, and he'd lost his shoes and his feet were cold. He was muddy, too, and the mud smelled rotten, and he couldn't quite rub it off. That, and wasps spun around him and he was allergic to stings.

So he convinced himself he was exploring, but went in ever closer circles to the house and back yard.

From the window of the second floor bedroom, Toby's mother and Anne watched him, amused. The school had called earlier to say he hadn't come in on the bus; frantic, Toby's mother had circled the block and nearly run headlong into Bernadine Boettcher. The two of them had talked, and in the middle of it, she had seen Toby rush across the street.

"He's funny," Anne said now.

"Isn't he?" Toby's mother said.

He was being careful at the fence, but the nettles grew high there, and he was not careful enough. The nettles stung and itched. He liked the smell, a resinous, green smell, but the itch was awful. He got his leg over and threw himself back and into the yard. He went around to the side and inspected the swallow nests. He poked under the maple, then dodged over to the utility shed, yanked the door open and went in. Inside it was suffocating and dry, smelled of acrid, moldy grass clippings and gasoline. It was darkish, there only being one small window. There was a small, key-sized hole in the ceiling to the rear, and a wasp climbed out of it. That did it. He opened the door and zig-zagged across the yard to the house. He stood with his back against the rough, sharp-edged brick. His stomach hurt terribly and he went around the stoop and sat, the kitchen window above and behind him.

She read to Anne from *The Wind in the Willows*, and when Anne was asleep, pulled a blanket over her. She went downstairs and into the kitchen. It was time now; she could feel him there. So she threw open the windows. She got out the mixer and the bananas gone bad. She cut and mixed. She put a teaspoon of nutmeg in her palm, and blew it out the window, through the screen.

He smelled spices. The mixer ran, bowls clanked, sliverware rang. He felt the saliva in the back of his mouth. His stomach rumbled. He turned to look at the door, the brushed aluminum storm door, the big, oak door behind it; and to the right, the door bell, long, slender ivory, like a piano key, set in black. All he had to do was push it. He struggled not to.

His mother hummed inside, then sang.

And if that mockingbird don't sing
Mama's gonna buy you a diamond ring

Doors opened and closed. When she ran the faucet the bird sang. There was a box for the paper, to the right of the stoop, and he balanced on it, and tried to see in around the big juniper. The tree was in the way and he couldn't see much. The cutting and mixing sounds went on and on. A cupboard door closed with a bang; it scared him and he nearly fell. The postman came up the street and he hid behind the juniper to the left of the door. The postman winked at him, and pushed the mail through the slot. His broad blue back went up the row of houses, until he turned at the end of the block.

"Bastard," Toby said. He liked that word. Toby liked the way the word rolled off his tongue. He sat on the stoop, and trying to think about something other than his stomach, and school, tested all his uncle's words. He tried new combinations. "Son of a bitch of a bastard," he said.

Then, excited, he remembered the back door, and the key under the mat. Sometimes his mother used it. He went around the house, and lifting the mat was surprised to see nothing there. Just scuttle bugs, running in all directions. He brought his bare foot down on them, then lifted it to see the damage he had done. It was anything but satisfying.

He strode along under the picture window awning. He tried the basement windows. He tried the porch door. He tried all the screens, even the one he'd rigged in his room, so he could get out evenings. Even that was locked.

He felt his face bloat, and marched around to the front door. He did not ring the door bell. Instead he got on the paper box, pulled back the juniper, and said,

"Let me in."

His mother appeared in the window.

"Hello," she said.

"Let me in," he said.

She tilted her head to one side, then the other, as if deciding something.

"You know how to ask for something, Toby."

Again he felt his face bloat. His face was hot.

"I want to come in."

His mother turned away from the window. The oven door creaked open, and he smelled banana bread. Toby loved banana bread. He took a deep breath, and said,

"Would you let me in, please?"

He could see the pans, the bread, cracked down the middle, the tops of the loaves lumpy and brown with walnuts and heavy with butter. He felt a sudden impulse to hurl himself at the door, but balanced on the box instead, quiet. His mouth watered badly. His legs ached from straining at the window.

"I got a call from the principal at the school," Toby's mother said cheerfully. "Were you at school?"

He had to think about this: if he told the truth, he would not be rewarded; and if he lied, and she caught him, that wouldn't be any good either. So he said nothing.

"You're awfully quiet," she said.

Still he said nothing.

"You must be hungry."

He hung from the window sill, watching. He hated her. He hated her and her bird and her stupid songs. He thought to punch through the screen. But he loved her too, and felt trapped.

"Let me in," he said. "I don't want to be out here anymore."

"Will you go to school tomorrow?"

His fingers felt raw on the brick ledge. His feet ached from standing on his toes. His stomach rumbled and his mouth watered; still, he hated the idea of school more than anything.

He watched her knock the loaves out of the pans. She arranged them on wire trays on the counter. She washed her hands and straightened things up. He smelled dish detergent, water, then banana bread again.

She went upstairs; an eternity passed.

"You deciding there?" she asked, back at the window.

"Where were you?"

"Waking your sister." She took one of the loaves from the wire rack, and in easy, gliding strokes, cut it.

"All right," Toby said. And under his breath said his uncle's words.

"What was that, Toby?" She glanced up, smiling.

"All right."

"All right what?"

"All right."

He could stand on his toes no longer, so let himself down, his back against the bricks; and anyway, it was easier like this.

"All right what, Toby?"

A car went by.

"I'm listening."

He stared out across the street. Old lady Dahlen was raking leaves. His stomach rumbled again.

"All right. I'll go to school," he lied.

"Good," his mother said, and opened the door.

·

He went through into the warm, banana bread-smelling kitchen. She did not ask about his shoes, or why his shirt was torn, or how he had gotten so muddy. She didn't ask him to wash up first, which surprised him and she didn't mention his father. She set a plate and three finger-thick slices of bread in front of him. He buttered them. The butter melted into the fine-grained slices. They tasted better than any he had ever eaten, flour and butter, walnuts and poppy seeds crackling in his teeth. He had one more, last, piece, and finished.

"Go get washed up," his mother said.

She kissed the top of his head and turned him toward the stairs. He went willingly now, though he had to boost himself up, step after endless step. And the following morning, at the bus, when it occurred to him to slip under the tree again and go skylarking, he thought he decided not to, and that was that.

Meeting Mr. Donatello

It was about the time my fathers cop friend Eddie stopped by I began to worry that I had, after all, committed some critical indiscretion. Eddie stood inside the doorway now, thumbs hooked in his Sam Browne belt, head nodding in that unctuous way of his.

"You understand what I'm gettin' at," he said. "We got that clear, right?"

My father, his broad back to me, nodded.

"Yeah, sure. Sure," he said. "But it had to be one of the other kids."

They argued at the door in whispers and I tried to listen from the living room.

On the sofa, I'd been watching the spring pre-season on the tube. Twins and the Royals. We were living in a rougher part of the Twin Cities back then, what was called Nord East, all Polish, Irish, and Black, and now, one Italian family, the Donatellos, and Eddie, nightly, was trying to keep tabs on things.

"They actually saw him, though," my father said. "That's what they're saying."

I tried to catch Eddie's eye, but he would not look at me. When he replied, emphatically, "*Yes,*" I felt something like electricity run up my spine. The tube there glowed in front of me, Harmon Killebrew at bat.

"A hunnerd percent sure. Close as me to your T.V. there."

I fixed my eyes on the set. I told myself what he was saying couldn't have anything to do with what I'd done earlier.

Then Eddie was gone, and here was my father, doddering around in the kitchen.

At the refrigerator he got out a can of Grain Belt, opened it with *ffft!* and took a long toot. He let go a deep sigh. He drank that can right down, then tilting his head back, his Adam's apple working like a pump, did another. He had big, solid arms—he worked at Calmenson Paper in St. Paul, on the dock—and flexed them, as though he were about to lift something heavy.

"Hey, Pauly," he said. "How 'bout a beer?"

This struck me as peculiar. But my mother was out at Garden Club, which was a sad irony, since we had no yard or garden, and here was the invitation I'd waited for for so long. I stood in the kitchen, a half-drunken grin on my face, while my father reached into the refrigerator for that cold, manly beer.

We were about the same size, but he was like rawhide from a life of heavy work. I was just seventeen, and would soon be off to the University of Wisconsin on a baseball scholarship.

My father, smiling—broad, friendly face, warm brown eyes—handed me that cold can of suds. I fumbled with the opener, trying to make it look as though this were a somewhat alien operation for me.

Still, I didn't exactly succeed. I guess I must not have wanted to. Maybe it was my way of trying to share this aspect of myself with my father. Athlete or no, I'd gotten to be a bit of a drinker.

I punched two holes in that can. Tossed back a fair amount, nodding stupidly.

"Looks like you really know your way around a can of suds there," my father said.

He seemed almost eager now to share in this camaraderie of beer I'd only known with my friends.

I shrugged. I was looking at the tattoos on his forearms. He'd served in the Big War, in the Navy, on destroyers. One tattoo was a heart with an arrow run through it, a drop of blood on the end. The other was a woman's name in the form of a snake, *Mary Lou*, which was not my mother's.

I took another tug at that can of beer.

"What do you say?" I said. I'd been hiding it pretty well up until then, how drunk I was. Under that buzzing, fluorescent light, I looked him in the eye.

"You and your pals take in that new movie tonight like you said you were going to?" he asked.

"Sure," I said.

He winked at me, and I winked back.

I didn't know he'd hit me until my head bounced off the wall, flash of blackness, and found myself falling, through a hell of a lot of space, onto the kitchen floor. I lay there with my cheek on the cold linoleum, blue-green speckles, and smudges of gray stuff swimming in my eyes.

I tasted blood.

There was my father's shoe, spit-polished to a black shine, inches from my nose.

"You know what I think about lying," he said. And stooping, he put his finger in my face. He was angry, but now, I could see, beneath that, he was frightened, too.

It put a chill in me.

I'd been heating up to go after him, but right there something went cold.

"You have really done it this time, buddy boy," he said.

Earlier, my friends, Mike Dougherty, Tom Wozjeck, and I had quaffed a few beers down at Culla's, a bar that served minors. Old Lady Culla had gotten to be a real friend to us, and we called her Mom, as some of the old timers did. Since this was our last spring together before we were all off—and victoriously, it seemed—to trade school for Mike, to a physics scholarship for Tom, and me, to Madison, Wisconsin, to pitch for the Badgers, Culla had spotted us a pitcher or two.

We were celebrating: We were out of this goddamned Nord East. We were smartasses, and pretty good at what we were up to. And that's the way the conversation had gone, walking back from Culla's, too.

It was late May, just after twilight, and the lilacs out, the grumble and whine of MTC buses (Metropolitan Transit Company) shaking us as we strode proudly toward home up Riverside and then to Franklin and 28th. Halfway up the block we'd stopped. There, big as all of life, was Mr. Donatello's Mercedes.

It shone there, to us obscenely, under the bluish streetlights.

The Donatellos had moved into the neighborhood the autumn before, taking the last of the old Pillsbury family homes, twice as big as the others around it. They hadn't mixed at all. They didn't mow their lawn themselves, rather hired help, fleetingly went here and there in the big Mercedes, and never lingered outside. It was only Angie, the Donatellos' daughter, we'd seen really. Angie, strikingly beautiful. She had the face of an angel, breasts that made your heart skip beats, molasses thick hair, and sparkling green eyes. She bustled by us on the sidewalk mornings, never so much as deigning to say hello; in fact, keeping her eyes on her shoes as she went by me.

And here was her father's car—her father, who was rumored to be connected to organized crime, and who none of us had ever seen.

"Jesus," I said.

"You can say that again," Tom said. "Check- it- out! What a set of wheels!"

We were looking at the car, but thinking of Angie. We were all more than a little smitten with her, but I'd taken it the worst. I was crazy for her, beyond all reason. Mike let go an exasperated breath. Ours was a neighborhood of dented green Pontiacs ten years old or older. Of bruised- blue Buick Roadmasters, all four door.

"You guys," Mike said. "You haven't got a clue."

"What?" Tom said.

"It's *family*," Mike said.

"Like what family?" Tom shot back. "Like our families aren't good enough or something?"

Suddenly we didn't feel so cocky. The car hulked massively beside us, almost as if listening. It was a Six Hundred, the biggest Mercedes made. Black and bulbous, and with that star on the hood, it smelled faintly of hot engine.

"Right," Tom said, a sneer on his face, "I mean, lookit this fuckin' car. Am I supposed to worship here beside the curb or what? Where's the fuckin' antenna?" Tom was drunkenly looking for it, I assumed to bend it over, or break it off. He'd done that to other cars.

"Electric," I said.

"Leave it alone," Mike said.

Tom was looking in the windows. "Lookit that maple dashboard and everything. I mean, who does this guy think he is?"

Still, we did not mention her. Mike was already easing up the walk.

"Come on," he said.

Tom spun on his heels and followed. A short distance away, he turned and hawked one on the windshield. Whistling, I snaked between the Mercedes and the Catalina in front of it, and without thinking, just like that, cracked the star off the hood.

"See?" I said, tossing it up under the streetlights and catching it. "Star light, Star bright—"

Just then, I thought I saw something move up at the house, but Tom, who was a good deal taller than me, ruffled my hair and whacked me on the back.

Mike just shrugged.

"You two clowns," he said. "What am I gonna do with you two, huh?"

.

I sat beside our Zenith, the Twins-Royals game playing, my father on the phone.

"Yeah, I know it," he said. "Yeah. Sure, sure."

I had plugged up my left nostril with toilet paper. When I pulled it out there was a long strand of clotted blood and my nose started bleeding all over again.

"*Can't* help it, George," my father said.

George was another policeman friend of my father.

Now I could hear George shouting back. It was a small, angry voice, but oddly all the more threatening coming out of the phone like that. My father never was one to swear, and to hear him at it nearly made me cringe.

"Put some ice on that," he said, suddenly turning to me. "Go on."

While I was in the kitchen, breaking ice out of the tray, his voice changed.

"How much?" he said.

I pulled back the handle on the ice tray. Set them in the yellow-checked washcloth. My nose was throbbing something awful. I didn't dare touch it, but thought, just maybe, it was broken. Holding the ice to my nose I craned my head around the kitchen door. My father hit the end table with his fist and the elephants my mother collected jumped in the air and fell to the floor.

"Don't gimme that shit, George." My father looked at me over his shoulder. "Right," he said. "But I can't undo it for the kid, see?"

A large part of my life I'd been waiting to see something stronger than my father bring him to his knees. It was just one of those boy things, one you get if your father's rigid or overbearing. But now that I was getting what I'd wanted, I didn't like it at all. It made me feel queasy, and what with the blood, and the pounding that had started in my head, I was half-doubled over.

"Not possible," he said.

Of course, right then, my mother had to come in. Pillbox hat and black suede gloves. She took one look at me in the kitchen, and another at my father, on the phone. He waved her away.

"Did you have an accident?" she asked.

I did not answer her. My father hung up the phone. He ran his hands through his hair.

"You're in for it, pal," my dad said, and motioned for my mother, now looking confused, to follow him into the bedroom.

While they argued, I called Tom. I was furious.

"You finked on me, you asshole," I said.

Tom denied it. My hand over the phone, I let him have it every way I could think of. I wanted to blame it on him, say he'd started it, looking in Mr. Donatello's car and all. But the more I railed at him, the more subdued and distant became his denials.

I called Mike. Just to imply, even through calling, that he'd finked on me offended him deeply.

"You'd better get your head screwed on straight, Paul. Because you, right now, don't know your eyeballs from your asshole."

At which point he hung up.

I got new ice for the dishtowel and thought to risk taking a look in the mirror over the sink. Sure enough, I had a black eye, and when I touched the bridge of my nose, I almost vomited. But, really, that is not what I'd gone into the bathroom for.

I could hear my mother's excited voice through the wall. Then there were three loud knocks. I flushed the toilet for effect, and went back into the kitchen.

I pulled out a chair and sat. The game was still on but I couldn't watch it.

The following morning, my father shook me awake. It was barely seven, yet he claimed he'd opened the lines of communication, as he put it.

So, what was I supposed to do?

An hour later, there I was, at the curb, with a bucket and sponge. Here was Mr. Donatello's Mercedes, badly in need of a wash and wax.

"Don't talk to nobody," my father said, gripping my shoulder. "And don't fuck around."

"Right," I said.

From the first I was aware that someone was watching me. I bent to it with the sponge, wetted the paint first, as my father had shown me to do with our Two twenty-five, which was ugly and had some kind of big chrome globe on the hood. If I looked at the Mercedes in just the right way, I could see the finest whirls in the paint, and that there was a clear coating on it of some kind. The sun came out, and it was hot, and bright, and the water smelled of lemon.

Kids went by on bicycles, laughing.

The neighbors across the street waved to me when I stood, poking each other.

.

"You missed there," my father said, pointing.

He was in his Navy blues, spit-shined black shoes. He stood behind me, smoking, as if nonchalantly, leaning against the elm. The paint, if anything, had gotten spotted with elm sap. I was working pretty hard to get it off. My hands where wrinkled as prunes.

"When you finish with that, you've got chrome to do," my father said, and then went back across the street.

.

Polishing that car I felt self-conscious. I even felt a bit of an actor. I really put myself into it, looked as industrious and well-meaning as possible, even though what I was feeling was humiliation. Right about noon, my father crossed the street again. He had something in his hands, and I thought, a sandwich.

It wasn't.

My father, armed now with screwdriver, vice-grips, and crescent wrench, reached into the grill of that car, then had the hood open. I knew Mercedes weren't supposed to open like that.

"Hey," I said.

"Shut up, you," my father said.

I looked across the street. My mother stood in the windows with her arms across her chest. I smiled at her but she did not smile back. Instead she let the curtains drop. I heard a match flair, and my father's eager sucking. He had that cigarette dangling from his lip.

"You know," he said, eyeing me, "I'd have you doing this if you wouldn't scratch the hell out of everything under here."

I still didn't know what he was up to.

He took what I'd thought was a sandwich and unwrapped it. A three pointed star, of course.

"Now you listen," he said, giving me a hard-eyed look. "This cost me a fair piece. I drove across town to Walzer Mercedes in St. Louis Park to get it. You're doing some work for me next month to pay for it. We got that clear between us? You understand?"

I said I did.

Finally, that car shone like a piece of obsidian in a rock store. Or, like the so-called "Navajo tear" my grandfather had brought back from Arizona for me. Or, just like my father's shoes. I stood back. My father did not touch me. Did not say, Job Well Done, didn't put his arm over my shoulder.

That car was perfect.

Even my father, master of spit-shined shoes, smudgeless brass cleaned in vinegar, of fingerprintless patent leather, could not find a blemish worth bothering with.

It was late, almost four.

"Done," I said, hefting the yellow bucket, and wax, and countless socks I'd ruined, polishing that monster of a car. I knew every inch of it.

My father chuckled meanly.

"Done?" he said, shaking that big head of his. "Nooo. I *don't* think so."

In the house, my suit was carefully laid out on my bed, even my bow-tie. I sat there, and when my mother came in, my oftentimes wedge between life as I wanted it and the way my father wanted it, she did not so much as address what this was all about.

"Your father wants you to put that on," she said, pointing to the suit.

I wanted to say, why? You tell me why? You tell me for what, and for who? But my mother, in her yellow dress, and her hair put up, a gold barrette across the back, answered all that for me.

"You know what you did," she said.

I did?

It was then, tired as I was, that I noticed the house smelled wonderful. Yes, simply that. My mother was a wonderful baker, and had made a chocolate cake. Two things came to me in a flash: first, I was angry: what did she think I was, a baby? That I needed this whole thing sweetened somehow? And secondly, did she think she'd get my father and me chumming up with a goddamn cake? And before we went *where*? My aunt's? For dinner? Always, when we'd gone, I'd refused to "be a little more formal," since it would only have been to impress my Aunt Betty's husband, this asshole doctor, but now I did that.

I dressed. I buttoned. I went into the bathroom and wet my hair down. I tried on a number of postures. I slumped. No. I stood with my chest out. No. I tried to effect a neutral posture. My face, boy, was that ugly. It looked like a baked potato across the bridge. My right eye was dark as a raccoon's. Quite frankly, I looked like some undertaker's nightmare. There was still crystallized blood in one of my nostrils. I tried to get it out, and damn it, if my nose didn't start bleeding again, which necessitated shoving some toilet paper up there, which made my voice all nasally.

But enough.

Here I vacillated between complete and utter rage, and a kind of terrified, but quiet contemplation of How Things Stood. My father had been a boxing champion in his days in the Navy, but here he was mooning around, smacking his fists in his hands, looking cowed in the living room.

It had to be pretty bad.

My mother, hovering, was trying to prevent yet another explosion.

"What's taking you so long in there?" my father said.

I shut the door. Flushed the toilet. Bent into the mirror.

"This is the last," I said.

·

But it wasn't. I was already looking forward to that cake, coming out of the bathroom, when I saw it on the kitchen table, in the big, tan tupperware container my mother always used when she was taking a cake somewhere, like up to my aunt's lake cabin. She straightened my tie, and stepped back. My father looked even more grim now than he had before.

I stood there dumbly.

"Here's the game plan," my father said, and there, even lovingly, he grazed my chin with his fist.

.

Crossing the street, balancing that cake in one hand, and clutching a half dozen roses in another, (in crinkly acetate plastic) I felt ridiculous. Here was Mr. Donatello's Mercedes, shining for all the world like a gem, though, already, slightly—only I, who'd worked on the damn thing all morning could have seen it—on the way to ruin, through the perpetual sprinkling of elm sap. Here the humped sidewalk, and, as I scaled the steps to the front door, here were the trimmed hedges and borders of well-tended peonies.

I stood at the door.

I was a robot. I was an emissary from I didn't know how many people. Who was this guy, that so many people should be afraid of him? And what was he doing in our neighborhood, Nord East of all places?

I reached for the bell but could not touch it.

I felt the eyes of my parents behind me. It was all insane. If things were so bad, why didn't the Donatellos just call the cops, or sue us or something? I thought. Through a certain act of contortion, balancing cake, and flowers, I managed to push the door bell.

It made a low, gonging sound inside.

My thoughts went back to the moment I'd snatched the star from the hood of Mr. Donatello's Mercedes. What had I been thinking? Nothing, I told myself, but that was nonsense.

.

The house was full of all kinds of smells. Aromatic smells. Baking smells. A musty smell. It was late, around dinner, and the woman who'd taken me in asked me to wait in a small, wood paneled room. She went off with the cake, but I held on to the flowers. I looked around me, waiting. There were bookshelves with leather bound books in red, and black, and gold. There were potted ferns hanging from the ceiling, and through the windows there, I could see the parted curtains in the front room of my parents' place across the street. I imagined my father watching another game in the pre-series. I looked at my watch; it was on, after all.

There were old photographs on the walls, and I looked at them, too. They were all inscribed, on the bottom, in Italian, not a word of which I understood. I noticed the rugs—velvety red and rich blue, Persian, even I knew that—and worried about my shoes.

What was taking so long? I was beginning to lose a bit of my composure. I didn't know Mr. Donatello, but now, waiting there, I disliked him more than a little bit, even conjured him up in a double-breasted, three piece suit and cigar, a big pinkie ring on one hand. Something right out of *The Untouchables*.

Finally, the maid put her head through the door. She wore an efficient looking white cap now, as if she'd been cooking, but it put me in mind of a hospital, and serious injuries.

"This way please," she said.

We went up a high, paneled hallway, jogged left, then up another, and finally stood on the threshold of the porch, in back of the house. There were hedges on all sides of the yard, even around the garage. It was nearly dark and going into twilight.

There was a long, narrow table there, in the porch, white tablecloth, silver candle sticks, wicker baskets of bread, and at the end of it, a short, balding, rounded-headed man in a blue dinner jacket.

Who, I assumed rightly, must be Mr. Donatello; at the other end of the table was his wife, a woman, who, to my surprise, was still lovely, even regal, in a loose hanging white gown. But what made my heart skip, and my eyes get heavy, was Angie there, in the middle, almond eyes averted, a shock of thick, dark hair over her shoulder, her mouth pulled into an embarrassed, red bud.

Mr. Donatello didn't lift his head to look at me. None of them did. The maid pulled out the chair opposite Angie. I wondered what to do with those flowers. I came down the steps, and something told me, Give them to Mrs. Donatello, and bow. Which I did.

"Thank you," she said, nodding slightly.

I stepped around the chair, and the maid pushed it bruskly up against my legs, so I as much fell onto it as sat.

Mr. Donatello motioned with his knife that I should take a roll. My mouth was dry, and even with a fair piece of butter on the bread, I could barely swallow. Mr. Donatello looked at me.

"Bit of a shiner you got there."

I nodded, realizing, right there, that my shiner was part of the reconciliation package. Mr. Donatello scratched the back of his neck.

"I hear you're going away next year?"

"To Wisconsin," Mrs. Donatello said, and actually smiled.

Mr. Donatello, who had swept his hair up from behind, as some balding men do, touched that hair lightly now, chewing. I tried not to look at Angie. Every time I did, I felt a kind of near hurt, but which was the most profound pleasure, also. I realized, then, I'd never seen a more beautiful girl, and that I was totally, truly, in love with her.

Mr. Donatello waved that little butter knife at me.

"Tell me you had a temporary lapse of judgment," he said, and took a bite from his roll.

It shocked me, how he'd just jumped into it. The maid filled our glasses with water.

"I did," I told him.

Angie, across from me, carefully ate a piece of green melon from her fork. There was a wet sheen on her lips. She was trembling.

"And why was that?" Mr. Donatello asked.

He ate his roll in small, mincing bites. His upper lip curled in what I at first thought was a sneer, but was in fact a gourmand's appreciation.

"Was it your buddies that got you to? Your pals?"

I considered his question, wondered what he wanted to hear.

"No," I said.

"Good," Mr. Donatello very nearly crooned. "Because that would have been a lie." He motioned with his knife. A basket of bread went around the table again. "Eat," he said. "Emanuella's rolls are very good, don't you think?"

Here I thought Angie inadvertently kicked me, and I pulled my legs off to one side.

The roll had turned to dust in my mouth, some unfamiliar spice in it, like licorice. The maid, Emanuella, set a plate of noodles in front of me. The sauce was delicately spiced, complex, with bits of purple in it, which I examined.

"Eggplant," Mr. Donatello said.

He tipped a bottle of wine over my glass, a deep, red wine, then slipped back in his chair, studying Angie, on his right, who glanced away.

"Do you hate us so much you want to do us harm?"

"No," I said.

"No?"

Mrs. Donatello smiled at me, graceful in her gown. There, again, was Angie knocking into me, but now, as if in some kind of code. She very carefully speared another piece of melon with her fork. Mr. Donatello opened his mouth, chewing.

"You're a baseball player, aren't you?"

"Pitcher, sir," I said.

"You like games, don't you?"

Now I could smell Mr. Donatello's cologne, a sweet, musky scent. It seemed to me almost flammable.

"You think you're pretty tough, don't you?"

"No, sir," I said.

"Isn't he tough, Angela?" Mr. Donatello put his hand on her forearm and she froze there. "She's been watching you and your pals out the windows evenings. Haven't you, Angela?"

Angela's face colored.

I settled in the chair, slouching. For just a second, her eyes focused on me, hurt, a kind of accusation there. But for what exactly?

"Isn't that right?"Mr. Donatello said.

Angie shook her head and looked at her plate. There was a fine pattern sewn into the collar of her shirt, a kind of silver filigree. Her

44

hands were lovely, long fingered. I felt an almost irresistible urge to touch her.

"It's not so much *what* you did that bothers me," Mr. Donatello said. He worked his knife in a vigorous, geometrical pattern over his pasta, cutting it. "That's nothing. It's *why* you did it."

"*Why*?" I asked.

Angela pushed the rind on her plate to one side. A buzz started up in my head. A bird was calling out there in the dark. Mr. Donatello turned that blunt knife one way and then the other, as if studying it, then suddenly looked at me askance.

"Yes. Why."

A number of excuses flashed through my head. Drunkenness. A random impulse. A key fob. None of them were suitable. Across from me, Angela did not stir. I wanted... I had wanted— I had wanted Angie to notice me, and she *hadn't*. And so I had... what? Tried to hurt her, in return.

But I couldn't say that. Especially not with her sitting across the table from me, and nearly shaking with what I'd mistakenly taken for embarrassment at my, all too obvious it seemed, infatuation with her.

Mr. Donatello, his eyes sliding around slyly, now faced me.

"Was it something to do with my daughter? With Angela?" he asked.

Now I know that, had he said it facing Angela, my answer would have been something other than what I did say. But Mr. Donatello understood that. He knew about ball players like myself, and daughters as beautiful as his. How to handle these matters.

"I want an answer," he said. "And then I'll let you go."

Let me go? I felt a flash of anger, and it occurred to me to say something ugly, to divert things, to give Mr. Donatello anything but what he was asking for.

He'd made me that angry.

"It was," I said, astounded even as I was saying it, "because *you're rich*."

Angela frowned, and my heart fell, understanding, in that instant, that what she'd been feeling hadn't been embarrassment over my attentions at all—no, but something quite the opposite.

But the damage was done. Mr. Donatello smiled a broad, victor's smile. Mrs. Donatello, at the end of the table sighed, having seen it all before.

"*Rich?*" Mr. Donatello said, laughing.

"Yes," I said, but already I felt a swelling in my throat. Oh, how wrong I'd been to say it! How weak of me to lie!

Mr. Donatello's laugh filled the small room, a booming, delighted laugh. When he'd finished that, he set his hand on the back of my chair, and eyeing his daughter across the table, said, in a hushed voice,

"You ever mess with my car again, you'll wish you'd never so much as seen it. Is that understood?"

I said it was, though I knew he did not mean the car.

.

Back at my parents' place, I came through the front door, into the living room.

"You look like you've seen the devil himself," my father said, oddly cheerful. "You learn your lesson over there?"

We sat in front of the television. The Twins were losing badly. It added insult to injury. I had a hollow the size of St. Paul in my chest, and worried I'd been done some strange and somehow permanent injury. My nose was nothing by comparison.

"Huh?" my father said.

"Do we have to talk about it?" I asked.

My father winked, a tough guy again. "Only if it doesn't take."

My mother stifled a sob in the kitchen. She'd seen how I'd gotten when Angela was around, and how Angela had always looked away, but it hadn't been any mystery to her what it was all about. *Men*— she was thinking, there at the counter. She said that sometimes. *Men.* Just that, and shook her head, as she did now.

I went into the kitchen and got myself a beer.

My back braced against the fridge, I drank it right down, and no one said anything.

In Less Than a Breath

I toss down another cup of coffee and push my chair back from the table. I want to stand, but I force myself to sit. My hands are shaking and my stomach is tight. "Never drink coffee before a meet," Jerry Schneider, my coach, has told me time and again. This is my fifth cup, and I may have another. I wish I would show some tangible sign of illness, but instead, I am so charged now that I can barely remain in my chair.

The North Face chalet is deserted. A half hour from now, the officials will close the ski jump and the coaches and competitors will come in for some "carbs"—Twinkies, or candy bars, anything for that last boost.

The high school kids will struggle and fight through the line first, the hoch team will follow, and then will come the veterans and the coaches in their Sorrels and tube-top parkas. I am on the hoch team, the high team. I wear the Minneapolis Ski Club's red and white jumpsuit and ski on the club's best equipment, though I haven't done so for long.

Until regionals last year, Kip Sorenson had the Club's top spot. Kip had been a hockey player and jumped like that, crazy and violent. On the thirty and forty meter hills no one could come close to Kip for sheer distance, and he knew it.

Kip jackknifed, bent at the waist over his skis, almost imperceptibly at first. When we moved to the Bush Lake sixty, and I began to match

Kip's distance scores, he pushed harder, and jackknifed worse. Jerry told me Kip would lose his distance advantage on the big jumps, the seventy and ninety meter.

And he did. I finally beat him at Chester, a jump in Duluth. He shook my hand after his last run, a big, lopsided grin on his face, and after that night we tied every other meet, Kip hurling himself always farther, while I held back, forcing my shoulders to curve over my skies and my arms to lie flat at my sides.

It went like that until early this month, when I got in two good runs at our central division tournament, and Kip was late on his second, nearly digging a hole in the crest of the hill with his skis. I picked up my trophy, an ugly gold-plated thing, then drove toward Highway Twelve on Wirth Boulevard feeling elated. At home I got a call from Jerry. The national team in Vermont wanted to see what I could do at Ironwood, Michigan, where a one-hundred-twenty meter jump had been built on Copper Peak.

"Don't get too excited," he said.

"Why do you say that?"

Jerry cleared his throat.

"Why did you—"

"I told them we'd think about it."

"What do you mean, 'think about it'?"

"Maybe by the end of this year.... Look, it's not like I said you don't have what it—"

"What did they think of Sorenson?"

"Maybe," he said, "maybe."

.

Jerry wanted me to wait—and even more so Kip—but we packed our van and went to Michigan anyway. The whole trip was a fiasco. On the highway heavy snow swirled around us like dense fog. Jerry pressed his face to the windshield, cursing in a low, guttural German. Kip sat beside him, cracking his knuckles, and I watched the yellow signs flash by from the back seat.

The first morning at Copper Peak, we sidestepped to the top of the landing hill, what's called the knoll, and back down, flattening the wind crust that had formed during the night. Then a jumper set the track, and the first man after him hooked over his skis and had to pull hard to keep his tips from dropping.

"It's damned fast," Jerry said, standing on the flats.

He shook his head. "You see that, Vogel? The whole track up there is black ice."

I said I'd noticed it.

Kip pushed his cap back and squinted into the sun. "Could slow down a bit, don't you think?" he said. He cocked his head sideways, then grinned, his eyes puckering under his brows, his lips twisting in the corners. I'd seen him grin like that coming back from a jump in Wisconsin once. Battle Creek it was called. We were tanked up on mad dog after a meet, howling down a back street of some nowhere town in Kip's '53 Biscayne, our wool suits stinking and the radio blaring Kip's favorite tune, Crocodile Rock. We passed a truck on a narrow bridge and Kip just railed right through, scraping our fender on the truck's bumper.

I turned around to see the driver of the truck stop in the middle of the road. He jumped out of the cab and shook his fist over his head and Kip turned to me and smiled that joker's smile.

"Good as, right?" he'd said.

.

Right. Good as a mile. I watch the waitress fill the cocoa dispenser behind the counter, then turn back to my coffee cup and poke at the brown grains in the bottom. I don't know what I'll say to Jerry and my teammate, Greg Halvorsen, when they come in, what excuse I'll use.

"Would you like a warm up?"

I'm surprised and jerk back in my chair. The waitress has her arm poised above my cup. She pours, my cup warms in my hand.

"Nice night for a meet, isn't it?" she says.

I nod and turn away from her, face the newly painted wall where my skis hang from a rack. Tonight they look like torpedoes, or bombs, or long blue bullets.

Since the accident, I've gone over my skis a dozen times, adjusting the heel blocks and cables. They said Kip should have come out of his bindings when he fell. But Jerry and I were watching from the bottom, and we could see that his staying in the bindings didn't have much to do with anything.

I rock back in my chair, anxious still, only this time I stand, then walk to the stairs and outside, my hands crammed into my pockets. Along the path to the jump the snow stands waist high, and a cold breeze rustles the dry and brittle leaves in the oaks. Flood lights from the hill cast hard-edged shadows across the path, and I can smell the kerosene heaters in the judges' box.

From there the coaches shout at jumpers in mid-flight.

"HANDS BACK!"

A jumper in a red suit darts by the judges' box and over the knoll. I check my step, listening. There is a hard, distant slap, plastic on ice, then the jumper spits out onto the flats.

The path widens and I climb to the crest of the hill. At the top of the scaffolding another jumper waits. Jerry yells from the judges' box, "LET'S SEE YOU HIT IT RIGHT THIS TIME, HALVORSEN!"

Halvorsen, high and tiny on the platform, waves for an all clear, gets it from the judges' box, then slams a ski against the backboards and rattles down the in-run.

His chest is too high, his legs too stiff.

"GET OFF YOUR HEELS!" Jerry yells.

Greg rocks forward, his ski tips pass the pine boughs, and late, he lunges out, "UNH!" jackknifing so badly he's got to pull his legs up under him so his skis don't nose into the hill. Then he drops out of sight, and there is that slapping of skis on ice. On the flats he turns to a stop, a rainbow plume jetting behind him. I clamber down the icy steps alongside the landing hill, hugging the rail, then wait at the bottom.

Out by the snow fencing that separates the flats from the river, Halvorsen shoulders his skis, then strides toward me and the stairs.

"How's it going?" I call to him.

He shrugs, but at the stairs, kicks the bottom step. "You saw it."

"You're looking better."

"Right," he says. Facing the landing hill, he talks through the side of his mouth. "Anyway... I thought Jerry was gonna get another toe-piece for your binding?"

There's no meanness in Greg, but he's always direct.

I nod, and Greg tugs at the strap on his helmet and glances in my direction, not quite meeting my eyes; then he mounts the stairs, his skis swaying on his shoulder.

Before the accident in Michigan, it was Sorenson, Halvorsen, and me. Teammates, all through high school. Every autumn Jerry had us run the lakes in town, and when the snow fell, we'd side-step the landing hills at Wirth, Carver Park, and Bush Lake, our legs shaking and lungs heaving. Then we'd ski down, practicing telemark landings, getting back the feel of our skis.

Our meets started in late December, with the local competitions, and ended the first week of March, with the regionals. We'd drive out to Wirth or Carver, or Bush five days a week those months, jostling each other, laughing, Kip singing Olivia Newton John songs I hated.

He did things you weren't supposed to do, and he got us doing them too. When Jerry drove the van onto the service road at Bush Lake, Kip ran behind and got a hold on the bumper, hooky-bobbing on his feet until Jerry stopped the van to chew him out. While Kip was getting a talking to, Halvorsen and I would scramble around the back and find a good place to hang on to. Sometimes Kip would buy cough syrup, the codeine stuff, and we'd all get stoned and go jumping.

He crashed a lot, but he got better.

At a new hill, Kip was always the first to take a run. Each hill was a surprise, each had some special characteristic: there was a drop-off in Eau Claire's out run, one that tossed you on your heels in the transition;

at Bush Lake, a hook in the scaffolding threw you off to the right side of the landing hill, near a stand of trees; and at Chester, a perpetual wind crossed the knoll, threatening to turn you on your side, mid-air, if you weren't careful.

Sometimes I told Kip he was an idiot. On bitter-cold weekends he'd call me.

"Let's go," he'd say. "It's ten fucking degrees below zero, Kip."

"So what?" he'd say, and I could just see his face.

Before kicking off the platform he'd catch your eye and nod, just once, as though he were tipping his hat. Then he'd slam off the platform, his arms held tightly in front of him, as though he were preparing to throw a punch. Gaining speed, he shifted from side to side, rocked on his squat legs to the bottom, then hurled himself off the jump and into the dark.

Like cutting glass, I'd hiss down the in-run after him, riding smooth over my skis, my body compressed and elastic. Toward the bottom I'd roll off the balls of my feet, and a hand's width before my ski tips crossed the pine boughs, I levered myself up and over the knoll. The hill dropped away then, and a great Ohhhhhh! hummed in my chest.

It happened so fast you had to get more of it—it was like a flavor, one you couldn't quite identity.

Something in it... exquisite.

Tournament nights, on the platform, you could smell hot paraffin from the jumpers waxing their skis; flood lights telescoped the length of the in-run like brilliant bluish pearls, and there was an utter stillness before each jumper's run. Down the scaffolding shadows spun about each jumper like hands on a clock, and from the landing hill, Jerry would yell, "HIYA! HIYA! HIYA!" dancing in his Sorrels. Sometimes my parents and sisters stood on the flats, and from the top I could almost pick them out of all the people clustered there.

After the meets we'd cruise Wirth Parkway, the windows of Kip's car open wide, Kip singing, our skis on the roof rack jutting over the windshield where everybody could see them.

Jerry is yelling again, his voice harsh, demanding. Halvorsen launches himself from the scaffolding, falling a good distance, his skis nearly perpendicular to the landing hill, a result of his jackknifing. He slaps down on the out-run and squirts through the transition, his hands braced on the snow behind him, another zero-style-point landing.

Out of the corner of my eye I can see Jerry is watching me. He leans out of the judges' box, his gloved hands clasped in front of him. I turn toward the chalet, scuffing through the snow on the path. A low oak branch snags my jacket and I tear loose from it. When I reach the back door, I jerk it open, pulling the return spring free with a snap! Behind the counter the waitress bustles, arranging candy bars and cakes on a long yellow tray.

The fluorescent lights glow blue and fuzzy, the walls press inward, and the air is stuffy and hot. I knock a chair back from the table nearest the door and sit, gripping the table top.

I feel like I'm falling through my seat, just tumbling end over end, like Kip in Michigan.

They said it was the sun, the sun had softened up the landing hill, making the snow a bit sticky there.

It was a headwind, pulled him off balance.

It was the fault of the bindings, their not releasing when he fell.

A ways past the five hundred foot marker, he met the landing hill in a telemark, smiling, his fist raised. But in the transition he was jerked backwards, his head striking the hill. A patch of blue ice.

And on the way out to Wirth this afternoon, in the van, while Jerry and Halvorsen argued about waxes, I unscrewed one of my toe-clips with my car keys and pocketed it. When we got to the hill, and hiked to the bottom, I noticed it was missing.

"You lost a toe-clip?" Jerry said.

I pressed the ski toward him, fumbling for something to say; his eyes went somewhere, far away from me, and then he climbed the hill to the judge's box. Watching his square, thick shouldered back move up the hill, I got the sensation of shrinking into myself.

That last morning, Jerry had argued with the national team coach, just yards from the flats.

"It's not a good time," Jerry said.

"Well, when will it be a good time?"

"This afternoon it might warm up. The track's pretty fast."

"I think you should send them down. Tell them to give it a sled ride the first few times."

"I'd like to think they could do that," Jerry said.

"Hell, my twelve-year-old boy's skied down the landing hill!"

"Maybe I'll have them do that," Jerry said, but I could tell he didn't want to.

Kip and I stood with our backs to them, looking at the jump. The landing hill alone had to be over seven hundred feet long, most of it a fifty percent grade or better, and above it, the scaffolding stretched to a tiny red point.

"What do you think?" I said to Kip.

Kip swung from side to side, from one foot to the other.

I breathed deep, the cold air sharp in my chest. "Don't go if you're not ready, Kip," I said.

He turned to look at me, frowning, his eyes narrowed.

Five jumpers in electric-blue suits stopped midway up the landing hill to pummel down a high spot. They moved in formation, raising and lowering their skis as though they were no heavier than shoes. The bottom man slapped the tail of his ski down and a hand-sized chunk of snow broke loose. It gained speed, then leaped high into the air and came down again and again, breaking into smaller pieces, all of them careening their way to the flats. The bottom man pointed, then spread his arms wide.

A second later the jumpers' laughter floated down to us.

"Assholes," Kip said. He balanced on the balls of his feet, his steel toe-pieces snapping through the hardpacked snow.

"Looks like quite a ride," I said.

Kip jerked his head in the direction of the landing hill. "They don't seem too impressed."

56

"No," I said.

"A few runs and we'll be right up there with those guys, what do you say?"

"It's big."

"Sure, it's big."

I looked at him askance and he stared back.

"I can do it," he said.

Jerry stepped away from the other coach and Kip glanced over at him, then turned back to me.

"Remember that first time you went off Chester?" he said.

I pulled my hat back, watching Jerry, who was nudging the snow with his boots, trying to decide something.

"Yeah, I remember," I said.

"Jerry said you looked like you were screaming all the way down."

I shook my head. We hadn't jumped Chester in two years, not since that night I beat Kip there. I liked Chester, but it was too small now.

"This isn't Chester, Kip," I said. "If you miss here, you're gonna fall a long, *long* way."

Kip blew a puff of air out his mouth. "Don't gimme that crap, Alex. I beat you a long time at Chester before any of this happened."

"Things change, Kip," I said.

Jerry came up behind us, and Kip turned sharply to him.

"You all set?" Jerry said.

The terrace door slams, and boots rumble across the ceiling toward the stairway. The Bernard fills with the jumpers and coaches, that frigid ashy smell of snow from outside coming with them.

Jerry sits with the coach from the St. Paul Ski Club, and Greg Halvorsen, poised between Jerry's table and mine, a Hostess fruit pie in his hand, turns in my direction.

"Got in some nice runs," he says.

I pick at my fingernails and shift in my chair. Around us the coaches and jumpers laugh, their voices thick with false bravery, and I feel a pressure in my arms, a desire to fling my coffee cup against the wall where my skis hang from the rack.

Halvorsen takes a bit of his pie and, shifting the filling to one side of his mouth, says, "You aughtta take a run before the meet. The track's real smooth." He swallows and takes another bite.

"Maybe I will," I say. I crush Greg's pie wrapper into a little ball and flick it off the edge of his table.

Greg clears his throat, then mumbles something through a mouthful of pie. I lean forward, and he says, "Shit...." He smiles, then holds out his pie. "See this?"

I look into the glossy filling, wondering what Greg wants me to see, and before I can pull my head back he shoves the pie into my nose.

"Very funny, Greg."

He laughs so hard his eyes glaze up.

"I don't think that's funny," I say.

"Christ, don't take everything so damn serious."

I hold my hands against my thighs and raise my head. "You weren't there."

"Right. And you aren't going to let me forget it, either. Are you?"

I push the table away and stand, then walk easy to the stairs. I pull my skis from the rack on the wall and heft them onto my shoulder. They weigh nothing. I know I should leave, now, before this thing in me is too big, but I am held back. At the table, Greg is perched on the back of his chair. Jerry is watching, too, a cup of coffee in his hand.

"Come on, Alex," Greg says, his arms outstretched, inviting me back to the table. "Jesus—"

I grit my teeth, holding it in, but the words escape me like a convulsion. "What the fuck is wrong with you?"

Greg's face reddens.

"You think his being gone is going to make you look better? Is that it? Is that the way you're going to get better?"

Greg stares off toward the counter.

"I'm talking to you, Greg."

The others huddle over their tables. Kip's death is no secret to any of them. Jerry pushes his hair back and stands, his face swollen.

"Fuck you," Greg says.

I feel my mouth twisting into what I know must be an ugly snear. "'Fuck you' is right!" I jab back. "If you had even half the guts—do you hear me, Greg?—it would take a miracle for you to even piss off a jump without falling on your ass. DO YOU HEAR ME, GREG?"

I charge up the stairs, slam through the back door onto the terrace. The stars are out, hard pinpricks of light above the oaks. I tear through the snow on the path to the jump and stand on the knoll, my hands clenched into fists. Nothing but nothing can come of this, I think. Nothing. Just a big hole where Kip used to be. And this club, this piss-ant club, the best I'd ever know.

Down on Wirth Parkway a car horn blares. Then there is that hush.

From the knoll, all of west Minneapolis spiderwebs out in patterns of yellow and blue lights. A pale reflection of the moon hovers over the river, just beyond the flats. A northwest wind blows, cooling my face. With the toe of my boot I chip through the icy crust in the center of the hill, feeling the layers, the giving way of crystal snow, and the ice again, unyielding.

The flood lights come on and the hill is a brilliant white ribbon set against a hillside of dark-limbed oaks. A judge scrambles around me with the marking chain. "'lo," he says. He pounds a spike into the top of the hill and stretches the chain down the landing hill. The caners shuttle by me, their poles held high. They position themselves all the way to the transition, where the flats spread into the darkness all the way to the river.

Halvorsen and Jerry climb the stairs from the chalet with the others. Jerry turns to me and says, "Your binding still on the blink?" He waits, long enough to shake his head, then slides down the hill to the judges' box, bumping against the embankment on the other side, Halvorsen following on his heels.

The night chill has set in, and a few latecomers take practice runs. Most of them jackknife: with their legs extended like stoppers, they crash down on the tails of their skis and ride the out-run to the bottom, hands braced against the snow behind them.

Jerry stares at me from the judges' box, looking more sad than angry now.

I pat the breast pocket of my jump suit, and feel the lump there.

Then, a jumper sets the track, and the meet begins. I hide from Jerry in the shadows under the scaffolding. Behind me, jumpers stand in line by number.

There is a ticking in the scaffolding, a rush of air, then a wooden slap! and an "Awwwww" rises from the flats. There must be a hundred and fifty people watching, from the sound of it. I know the last man has fallen, has gotten zero points for style. I wait to hear his distance P.A.'d from the judges' box.

One hundred and sixty feet.

On a clean, fast night like tonight, I can break one ninety five on this jump. Kip could do better than two ten.

The scaffolding rattles again. Then again, and Halvorsen, his back to me, is on his way up.

I carry my Elans to the tool boxes on the Bernard side of the jump, and heft a piece of paraffin from the box nearest me. On my right, a jumper melts wax with a butane torch, touching up his skis. The smell puts me on top for a second, on the platform, where I can see for miles. Then there is the sensation of motion. But it fades, and I can't get it back. I turn my skis over and run my hand down the P-tex bases. Under the floodlights the bases glow a warm yellow, but are slick and cold to the touch. In sharp, even circles, I force the wax into the bases. Then I am hammering at them, whacking the bases with the paraffin block, leaving big, sticky swatches of wax.

There is that smell again, that sense of motion.

I won't stay down here anymore, sick with fear and wanting. I pull the toe clip from my pocket and twist it back into the binding with a screwdriver. The screwdriver blade skips out of the toe piece, poking my hand so it bleeds. I rub snow into the cut, then pull on my gloves and check my heel blocks and cables. I shoulder my skis and step into line, then climb the scaffolding. From there everything looks so small, the pebble-sized upturned faces, the strip of snow through the oaks narrowing to a point.

Then I am on top with the others, swaying in the wind, pumping my skis back and forth to shake the stiffness from my legs. The sky bulges from the point where I stand. There is that smell again, hot wax, and a cool wind on my face.

The jumper before me is off, and I step into the center track. It is as though I am watching myself from a faraway place.

A hundred faces are raised below me, white hollows with dark centers, and the horizon yawns wide and dark from the end of the jump. A chainer waves the all clear.

The scaffolding shifts and groans in the breeze.

I snap my right leg back, the ski hits the backboard, and I slide out and over the edge of the platform, dropping, WHHOOMP! onto the steep in-run. It is as if my head is being pulled off, the blackness and lights and trees and faces bursting through me. And faster, everything is sharp, intense, as if packed with light, distorted with speed and height, compressed below, lengthened at my side. I shift forward, my chest riding elastic above my legs. The support beams whoosh, whoosh, whoosh by, my legs somewhere beneath me, they know what to do, and now the ramp curves out and the pine boughs rise up, grow larger, and the two tracks there gleam, and my skis damp and smooth, and I roll forward, feel myself falling, and at that moment I burst off the ramp. A brilliant white flash nearly blinds me, and everything in me says, STAND UP! as the knoll drops out from under me, but I lay out over my skis, and the air buoys me up, and I push further into the horizon, head out, arms at my sides, the faces below glowing, and I fall a long, long distance, forever it seems, weightless, skimming on a sheet of air, and at the last possible moment, when I will be crushed on the hill if I do not land, my legs pull under me, my skis meet the hard snow in a slap, and in the transition, like coming up the next rise on a roller coaster, I am pushed down, then shot out onto the flats, standing now, gliding toward the river, all of it singing in me.

2

What We Do for Love

Spice Rack

He was bumping at the door, trying to get his key in the lock, the spice rack hugged awkwardly to his middle, when, to his surprise, the door began to open by itself. There was that cher-clock of the dead bolt, and the scrabble of the safety chain.

Artie thought to jog back to the car to hide the rack in the trunk, or, to set the rack alongside the house, where he could bring it in later. He shifted on his feet, precious seconds passing. But no.

The door swung wide.

Over the rack, Artie grinned, broadly, preparing to do what he must. He would say, *Darling, Happy Valentine's Day! Sorry you caught me getting it into the house. You weren't supposed to be nome. Really!* But it was not Artie's wife who stood in the door; it was Artie's mother, Beatrice—Bea, for short—her hair in pink curlers.

Artie, his scalp tingling, rushed by her, pretending business. He caught the spice rack on the countertop corner, before heading clumsily down the basement stairs.

"What have you got there?" his mother said. "Be careful, you're scratching it!"

Now Bea sat on the sofa, poking a strand of hair back into place, struggling to conceal a smile. She had seen the spice rack, of course, but she wasn't about to say so. But why was she grinning like that?

"Enough sugar?" Artie asked.

"Certainly," Bea replied. Artie dropped another cube into his mother's cup. He knew she hated that. She was a little over five feet tall, and pushing two hundred pounds, but sweets she could not deny herself, among other things. Having Artie push them on her, as she thought of it, made her furious. Still, Artie knew she could not refuse.

"So," Artie said.

"I'm helping Carol clean," Bea said matter-of-factly. She had cheeks like apples, and they very nearly shone with feigned good intention. Carol, Artie's wife, hated Bea's dropping by unannounced, "poking around" she called it. Artie knew it was just some strange battle between them.

"You were," he said.

"Yes. Remember? You asked me to?"

Earlier in the year, when Artie and Carol had gone out of town, they had given Bea keys, so she could check on the house and, now, Artie had come very much to regret it.

"I thought you might just be snooping," he said.

Bea eyed him over the rim of her cup. "Really, Arthur," she said.

Artie nearly laughed. *Arthur.*

"And," Bea added, "You'd best not forget Valentine's day. It's Wednesday, you know. I'll never forget how hurt Carol was last year."

"Don't remind me," he said.

Artie, every year on Valentine's day, bought Carol a dozen roses. Last year, he'd gotten the days mixed up somehow, and Carol had been more than upset.

Sinking into his chair, Artie let go a deep sigh. Bea sipped her tea.

"Arthur?" she said, but Artie was far away.

.

Weeks before, Artie had taken his mother to Schramm's, a fine furniture outlet, where they had first seen the spice rack. It was *not so dear*, Bea said, fondling the price tag and making doe eyes at her son.

"Look at the fine work. Do you see things like this anymore?" she asked.

The rack was impressive. It was an antique, adorned with hand-painted prairie flowers—asters, and blue bells, and black-eyed susans. Artie found he actually liked it himself. The two of them had hovered over the rack, mother and son, though Artie was thinking of Carol.

Scrabbling in the cupboard one afternoon she'd said, angrily, "Why is it we still live like this?" She was trying to find the ginger. The spices were all thrown together in a drawer, hand-labeled on masking tape, in small bouillon jars, a remnant from Artie's bachelor days.

Every year Carol would complain about the spices. It had become one of those silly things in their marriage: who would put the spices in order.

"Do you think your father would like it?" Bea asked.

"Dad?"

Artie's father hated old things: he was a gadget man. New, shiny. Out with the old. In with the chrome and glass.

"Wouldn't he love it?"

Like a quintuple bypass, Artie thought.

"Let's pick up your chair, all right?" he'd said, taking his mother's arm and steering her toward the back of the store.

But the spice rack stuck in his head. Somehow, the very fact that it was overpriced, and was ridiculous for what it was—too big, too many compartments, too much decoration—made it desirable. He even found himself thinking dear, his mother's appellation for everything from Holly Hobby Dolls to Champagne Music to grossly cheerful holiday decorations.

Artie hated all that. But the rack tagged along with him, an irritation, much like a beer jingle couched in an all-too-catchy melody.

Nightly, the following week, while Carol and he watched television, or fixed dinner, Artie had thought about the spice rack. In the kitchen, he would have to drill holes in the wall. But where?

"What are you thinking about?" Carol asked.

The space between the cupboards was perfect.

"Nothing," he said.

"Work again," Carol said.

"Yes, of course," Artie had answered.

"You're not listening," Artie's mother said.

"I heard every word," he replied, which was a lie.

"What did I say then?"

Artie grinned. "It was your hip. Or was it that Ferguson woman at the grocery? The one who needs a good talking to? Or grandma Ziegler? Or the price of hams in 1945?"

Bea drained her cup and set it carefully on the table, even lovingly.

"You were always a funny boy," she said.

Artie was dumbfounded. Funny? Was he mistaken, or was she smiling to herself? Yes, she was. A self-satisfied little smile. There it was again.

It made his scalp crawl.

"I'll see you for my birthday the week after next, right?" she said coyly.

Artie blinked. In that moment, the whole thing, in all its messy complication, came clear to him: His mother had not only seen the spice rack when he'd dodged in with it, but seemed to think he'd bought it for her!

Artie eyed his mother evilly.

"More tea?" he asked, dropping another sugar cube into her cup.

At Schramm's, he stood under the hot display lights looking at a new spice rack where the old one, the one he'd bought, had been, trying to calm himself. The new rack was without charm, was even ugly. Artie called over a sales person. She wore an efficient-looking three piece suit, and smiled in a calculated way he didn't like.

"Can I help you?" she asked.

They talked for a few minutes, in which time Artie worked out of this *Nancy* that, even though the rack had been an original, it had not been an antique; no, even the label had stated that plainly, *antique finish*. It had only been shaker *style*, the girl told him.

Artie felt a flair of anger. The whole thing was ridiculous. Why didn't he just tell his mother the rack was for Carol? Period.

"If you want, you can return the rack for a cash refund," the girl said. Already she was taking a note pad from her breast pocket.

"No, no," Artie told her. "I'm looking for another. Just like the one you had here before. You know what I mean?"

The girl's eyes brightened. "Yes," she said. "I mean, we could have something built."

"Won't do," Artie said. "Need it by the 28th."

The girl rapped her nails on the notepad. Fuchsia. She rambled on about suppliers and something about New York or Vermont and special wood. Artie asked her what she was trying to tell him.

"There are others," she said. "In back."

"Others?"

Valentine's day went beautifully. As he had hoped, Carol was thrilled with the spice rack. There were kisses and chocolates and expressions of delight. Now the expense of buying two racks seemed more than justified.

"Put it up" Carol said, holding the rack to the wall. In the light, Artie could see the scratch he'd made rushing with it into the basement earlier. A gouge, really.

He felt himself blushing. He was afraid she might think, *damaged*. And there would be another battle.

"Oh, it's *perfect*," Carol said.

Artie explained that he'd have to find the studs in the wall. He'd have to go to the True Value to find the proper hardware. As he said it, he was surprised to find he was sweating.

"I like your hardware," Carol said, and taking his hand led him out of the kitchen.

All that week Artie suffered. He could not have Bea in the house, not yet, so he offered to sit a friend's cat, Chester, that howled in their basement nights. Bea hated cats, so the cat kept her away. And he painted the bathroom, another thing to keep his mother out of the house. The fumes give you brain damage, Bea told him over the phone. When the cat was gone and the paint dry, Artie invited his mother to lunch at Wang Ming's House of China, where he suffered through plates of greasy sweet sour pork and Hot and Spicy Number 7, which was a concoction of exactly what he could never tell.

All of it would have been unendurable but for Bea's seemingly indestructible cheer. She talked about the orchids she'd bought, and the texture of the potting soil, warm and soft and with that wonderful dirt smell, she said. Her hands dipped and turned over the table. With a sparkle in her eye, she mentioned Artie's father.

"Dad said that?" Artie asked. "He wants a second honeymoon?"

Bea grinned shyly. "You'd be surprised what a little gift can do."

·

At the end of the month Carol threw a party for Bea in her home, as she'd requested. Bea had invited a number of her friends, more than Artie could have imagined. They tooted horns, turned noise makers, and wore brightly colored foil hats in the shape of animals. Carol led them in a round of "Happy Birthday" and "For She's a Jolly Good Fellow." Finally, after having opened her other gifts, Bea got to the spice rack. She paused, just a second, then ripped the paper from it.

"Oh, Wonderful!" she said, her eyes glassing up.

Artie's father winked at him from the couch.

It was all wonderful, except for Carol's pinching him, and after, driving home in the car, Artie had no trouble telling Carol half the truth, which was, unfortunately, also half a lie. "She saw your rack there on the wall and liked it so much I thought, what the hell—if it makes her happy I'll get her one, too. My mother could use some happiness, you know?"

Carol looked at him askance.

"You're wonderful," she said, a little ambiguously, and Artie forced himself to grin.

"You too," he replied.

·

The week following, at the office, he put it out of mind. When it did come to him, the spice rack business, he smiled, and just as quickly shook his head. He had been lucky getting out of that mess, after all. Desk, papers, the phone ringing. He was busy and back in the flow of things. Disaster had been averted. Bea did not visit the house. Carol had thrown herself headlong into her work at the Civic Center downtown, where she coordinated events, and time went by like that.

Bea and Artie's father vacationed in Mexico. Thanksgiving came and went uneventfully. Nearly a year passed, and everyone seemed happy.

Yet, there was something nagging Artie:

It was an accident, that he'd extended himself the way he had. It had worked some kind of magic, in the end, and he was grateful for it, but uneasy.

After all, gifts, in his family, had a way of coming back at you.

.

A week before Christmas, Bea called to say she was bringing something over. Artie and Carol waited in the living room for her. Here, now, the tree was up. The lights blinked off and on, blue and green and red. Tinsel hung down over the picture window, sparkling. A light snow was falling outside. Then there was the ding-dong of the bell, and Bea, thrilled with herself, all cheer and ceremony and pomp, came in. She knocked the snow from her boots, called, "Hello hello hello!" and pulled the door closed behind her, all the while balancing a plastic-topped tray against her bosom.

"Well," she said.

Carol motioned her over to the sofa. Bea stooped, as if to sit, then remembered the tray.

"Oh," she said. "I brought some pfeffernusse."

Carol asked what pfeffernusse was and Artie explained. They're pepper cookies, he said. His mother hadn't made them since he was a boy. It was more of that magic.

"I'll just set them in the kitchen," Bea said.

Artie's scalp crawled. But why?

He told himself it was nothing: just nerves. He'd explained to his mother that Carol had seen the spice rack that night at the birthday party and had wanted one just like it. This many months later, who would care who had gotten theirs first?

Who could tell?

Behind them the kitchen light came on. Artie craned his head around. There, Bea, his mother, bustled at the table, humming to herself. She'd even brought green and red napkins, was arranging the pfeffernusse on a silver tray to carry into the dining room. She nodded her head happily, and then, just as she was about to lift the tray, stopped. Just that.

Artie's heart leapt.

Bea stared up at the spice rack. She'd seen it tens of times, but some dark thing crossed her face now. She reached out, and with her index finger, felt the length of the scratch. Her mouth dropped open. Right there, under the light, it seemed her hair grew brittle, her face went slack with age.

"Mother," Artie said.

In a rush, Bea strode to the door.

"*Mother*," Artie said again.

"I forgot something," she blurted and went out.

Artie got his coat from the closet.

"What's going on?" Carol asked.

"Nothing," Artie replied.

He pulled on his shoes and chased after his mother, who'd reached her car now, a big, red Lincoln Continental.

"Mother," Artie shouted.

There was the slam of the car door, the motor gunning, the car pulling away from the curb. Artie caught the door handle, running along with the car. Inside, his mother hunched over the wheel, sobbing.

"Stop *dammit*!" he shouted.

The car gave a quick jerk, throwing Artie off, then sped toward the end of the block, and there, after narrowly missing another at the intersection, horn blaring, turned and was gone. Artie bent down, his hands on his knees. He was dizzy, sick.

"Artie?" Carol said, standing behind him.

The snow was falling heavily. It made a subtle hush. Artie coughed; spots swam in his eyes.

"Artie," Carol said, "Whatever it is, it can't be that bad. Artie?"

He turned to look at her. The lights in the picture window blinked off and on. Carol wrapped her arms around him, subtly squeezing. Her cheek was cold and dry against his.

"Come on, Artie," she said, "it isn't that bad."

Artie, struck dumb, could only nod

Yes. And *Yes*.

Swimming Lessons

S o, you going to sulk all afternoon?" Joe Price asked, teasing.

Claudia, Joe's wife, shrugged From where they sat on shore, eating lunch on a plaid blanket, they could see the boats going by. Skiers. A sailboat listing to one side further out. It was late August, and hot. Claudia twisted her red hair up over her head, knotting it.

This was not a good sign.

The Prices were on vacation, something they'd looked forward to all summer. It should have been wonderful, just the two of them, without all the distractions, their children, business, housekeeping, but now, some balance had been upset.

Joe watched his wife's fingers work her lovely hair into place.

Earlier, on the par nine, when he'd offered a bit of advice on how she could improve her swing, by changing her grip, she'd offered to wrap her club around his neck.

It worried him.

"Hey," he said. "Arnold Palmer."

"What?" Claudia was squinting into the sun. But still, he'd made her smile.

"Beat you into the water?" Joe said, meaning, How about a swim?

Claudia grinned, then kissed him on the forehead.

"I win, we see a movie tonight."

Joe considered this. He knew what movie his wife was thinking of. He had no interest in driving all the way into Farnsworth to see that four hanky tear-jerker. But Claudia was always slow to get moving, even *glacial*, he thought.

"All right," he said.

Like that, Claudia was up off the blanket, running headlong toward the water—and seeing what she was up to, Joe charged after her—both of them, sprinting now, both dressed, Claudia jumping over a woman stretched on a recliner, "Oh, My!" making for the water, shock of droplet diamonds around her legs, Joe taking a big hop, skip and a jump, across the strip of sand that separated him from the lake, coming down belly first with a wet slap!

Joe jumped up, looking around him.

"Beat cha!" Claudia shouted gaily from where she stood further out, her dress revealingly plastered to her, a mosaic of wet cloth and skin.

Joe set his hands on his hips, glaring.

But then he laughed. "All right," he said, but he did not say *you win*.

.

Back at the cabin, in the screened in porch, the night sounds loud around them, Joe couldn't seem to shake the mood of the movie. It had ended, tragically, with the hero, a woman, dying of cancer. Helpless. He sipped at his drink, Claudia's head in his lap. He kicked the glider back again, swinging. He liked the scent of Claudia's perfume: rain.

"What are you thinking?" Claudia asked.

"Nothing," he said. But he was thinking of how she'd tricked him.

"Quiet without the kids around."

Joe took another pull at his drink. "Sure is," he said.

Thinking of Toby, and Anne, he felt vaguely afraid. Usually, he was so busy he didn't have time to think about much. Things just seemed to go. You worked, paid the bills, did all the things you were supposed to do, and if you did it right, *voila!* happiness was to follow.

Now Toby was a disciplinary problem at school, and Anne was quiet and withdrawn.

They had agreed not to "bring the kids" along, but here they were. Invisible. Front and center.

"What are *you* thinking?" Joe asked.

"I'm thinking of... a big, juicy watermelon," Claudia replied, ruffling Joe's hair. "*You.*"

.

In the bedroom, later, he was not altogether comfortable with her inventiveness. He felt strangely cut off from her and alone. In the past few years they'd always been pressed for time.

He didn't know what to expect now.

There was something nearly desperate in it, their coupling, and it filled him with a deep and disturbing sense of something unpleasant to come.

And, too, where had she thought of all that?

In a rowboat, the following morning, up a small inlet at the north end of the lake, Joe reached for Claudia's line.

"Here," he said.

"I'll do it myself," Claudia replied.

She was almost charmingly disheveled. Sleepy. Her fine hair rumpled in a blue scarf. Claudia was not a morning person. Her hands fumbled the line into a complicated series of monofilament loops.

Joe sat against the motor, humming. A mist had risen on the water, and the sun was low over the trees. Claudia still wasn't having much success.

"Five times," Joe said.

"*What?*"

His heart kicked. Had he said something? Five times?

A blue heron churned slowly and gracefully by out on the lake and was gone. Joe reached for Claudia's line again.

"Don't," she said.

"You put the line through the leader and loop it around five times. Like this."

Joe demonstrated with his rig.

"See?" he said.

"I can do it myself," Claudia said, clutching the line to her breasts.

.

The week went on interminably.

It seemed that with a certain regularity she snapped at him now. Look, he said, watching her make the coffee. If you overfill it, the grounds go over the side and into the pot. See? When she fumbled with one of the deck chairs, trying to get the back to stay up, he intervened, showing her how the ratchet worked. Again she snapped at him.

Do you think I don't know how to use a deck chair?

I didn't say that, Joe said.

How much he did not say, he did not tell her. When she swam the breaststroke, for example, which she seemed to be so proud of, she did not properly synchronize her kicks. After dark, she always turned the lights of the car on before she started the engine. He told her about the alternator, and how it worked, how turning the lights on before the engine drained the battery, but that got him nowhere. This is how I start the car, all right? Claudia said. When she was sweeping up one morning, he saw how she worked almost at random. *And* she gripped the broom stick queerly, both palms on the same side.

What are you looking at me like that for? she said.

Nothing, he'd replied.

.

Toward Wednesday of that week, swimming as often as they did, Joe finally gave in and thought he'd give Claudia a few swimming lessons. She'd been on the swim team in high school, and he wondered how it was no one had ever pointed out her strange kick.

It was afternoon again, and they were in the water, at Claudia's insistence, a little sooner than they should have been. On the beach were kids with blue and red inner tubes, waiting to get back in, their mothers slathering themselves with lotion. A few men smoked back of them. Joe got out of the water, to watch Claudia.

"Honey," he called.

"She's a real dolphin," the man beside Joe said.

Joe nodded. He talked with the men there, making them laugh. He watched Claudia in the water. She was paralleling the shore. She moved powerfully from one end of the swimming area to the other—but not as powerfully as she might—then ducked under the water, at the yellow buoys, and turning, headed back. She seemed not to hear him, and so he raised his voice.

"*Sweet*heart!" he nearly shouted.

When that failed, he strode into the water, determined to do the good thing, unpleasant or not. Claudia stood, knocked her head from side to side to clear her ears.

"What do you want?" she asked.

Copper-red hair over creamy pale shoulders dotted with freckles. Ring of cobalt blue suit over her breasts. Those piercing green eyes, fierce.

"What?"

"It's about your kick," Joe said.

The remainder of that afternoon Claudia cried, and over the smallest things. When Joe said, Next year, why don't we go down to Mexico? she burst into tears.

Just go away for a bit, will you? she said.

Joe obliged her.

He went down to the dock, and there, in the bright sun, read the flyer the owner of the resort had given them. There were horseback riding, tennis, and the tandem bicycles they hadn't gotten to yet. A Viking runestone in town, at a small museum, and an all resort campfire.

Humming, Joe got out a pen, and on the backside of the flyer began to make lists. He divided the sheet into *House, Toby/Anne, Office*. In a fourth column, he wrote, *Vacation*. He studied the front of the sheet, ordering the activities with small circled numerals.

If they worked things just right, they could get most of it in yet.

Late afternoon, almost dusk, on the last day of their vacation, Saturday, and Claudia had burrowed under the covers and refused to come out. Joe sat on the edge of the bed, trying to coerce her into taking the Sunset Ride—which he'd already signed them up for.

"Tell me why not?" he asked.

He could just see the tip of Claudia's nose and a wedge of red hair under the covers. Her nostrils flared.

"Because I don't *want* to," Claudia said.

"Think of it," Joe said, "the sun going down, the horizon kind of backlit... a campfire."

"I said 'no,'" she said.

"But why?"

"*Because*," Claudia said.

"Because isn't—" He was trying not to mention the expense.

"If you don't shut up, I'll scream. I really will."

"Claudia—"

There came a muffled sob from under the covers, then cursing. "Can't you ever just *leave things alone*? Do you always have to be *messing* with everything?!"

"What do you mean, *messing*—"

The small room was filled with a high-pitched, ululating wail. It made Joe's ears ring. When it stopped he shook himself.

"Listen—"

"I'm warning you," Claudia said.

Joe lifted the curtain from the window beside the bed; just off shore, two men fished in the reeds, casting. It seemed terrible to spend their last night here in the cabin.

"How about we row out into middle of the lake later, watch the moon come up?"

Claudia shifted under the covers. She stretched, deciding something.

"You'd like that?" she asked.

It was very nearly balmy, in the eighties still, and dusk was upon them. Joe, rowing the small, wooden boat, had worked up a sweat. He enjoyed the rhythm of the rowing, and bent to it. Claudia sat against the transom. They were a fair distance out, the swells larger, the lake glossy black and immense, the shoreline distant, the lights coming on in the cabins there.

Joe dipped and pulled at the oars. They had eaten a fine dinner in town, and Claudia had dressed in a flimsy, gauzy dress. There was something almost medieval about it, Claudia's dress, rowing, the warm yellow light in the windows of the cabins on shore.

Seeing Claudia there, beautiful and otherworldly, her surprise that first morning, fishing, came back to him. What had that been all about?

"Can I?" she asked.

They traded places and Joe sat against the transom, watching. It was obvious she'd never rowed before, didn't know how to feather the oars.

"You've got to aim them," he said, turning his hands down and in.

Claudia smiled. "Like this?" she said, doing the opposite.

He watched her for a time. "If you're so smart, then why don't you do it right?" he asked sharply, and knew, immediately, he'd said the wrong thing. Claudia quietly set the oars in the boat.

"Do you want to swim?"

"Sure," Joe said.

He tugged off his shoes, got out of his clothes, and lowering himself over the transom, winked at Claudia. He would jolly her.

"Nothing better," he said, determined to get things back on track.

Turning in a lazy circle on his back, he found Cassiopeia, a W shaped constellation, and felt pleased with himself. He let his arms hang down, bobbing there. When he tired of waiting, he lifted his head. The boat was a good distance away.

"Hey!" he shouted. "I'm over here!"

Claudia hauled at the oars, moving further across the lake.

"All right. Real funny," Joe said, laughing. "Come on now, you joker."

Claudia did not stop.

"Claudia," Joe said, trying to keep his voice steady. "What are you doing, sweetheart?"

He was full, and the drinks he'd had over dinner made him feel more than a little sluggish. Claudia worked the oars clumsily, widening the gap between them.

"This isn't funny, Claudia," Joe said.

He threw himself across the water, and when he reached the boat, tried climbing over the transom. Claudia hit his right hand with an oar. For a second, he floated, yards back.

"Claudia," he said.

He felt a bit of nausea. His hand throbbed. He worried he might vomit. He spun around; the shore was distant, the lake seeming depthless, dark, sucking him down. He felt his face bloat, said,

"It's about somebody else? Isn't it?"

"No," Claudia said. "It is not about somebody else."

Joe took that in; he didn't know what to feel. His legs sunk down, chilled.

"What if I were to shout for help?"

Claudia cocked her head oddly to one side, working herself up to something.

"Yes, why don't you?"

Joe made another dash for the boat, and Claudia hit him with the oar a second time, harder.

"*Claudia*—"

"Shout," she said. "Go ahead. Show them that something's wrong."

Joe made for the boat again, and Claudia, working the oars with a crude, and angry efficiency, stayed just beyond his reach.

"*What* are you doing?" Joe shouted.

Around and around they went. Joe cursing under his breath, Claudia staying just beyond him. "You could move a little faster, if you cupped your hands tighter," she told him. "Try your kick. One two, one two," she said, echoing what Joe had said earlier. After a time, Joe tired.

"Listen to me," he pleaded. "Please, please, please, just *listen*."

Claudia sat up; the oars trailed in the water.

"What?" she said.

Joe pulled himself over the transom in back. He was too exhausted, too sick, to be angry. He sat, hunched over, trying to get his breath back. Claudia, as if chilled, hugged herself. A fat, red moon was rising. It cleared the trees, then hung, like an immense lantern, over the lake.

Now Claudia was rowing again. Joe felt himself lean toward her— *don't cock your wrists like that*, he thought to say—and just as quickly sat back.

"What?" Claudia asked.

"Nothing," Joe replied, affecting a smile, "It's nothing at all. Really."

Stealing Time

I get this creepy feeling lately, that I want to steal things. Or it isn't even a feeling. I'm in a hardware store, and I think, *lean over and grab a handful of washers from that bin, Curtis.* It makes no difference that I don't need the washers. At the supermarket, I eat an apple in the aisles, or pour a handful of Cajun Crunchies into my palm and swallow them whole.

I want to take things, without paying for them. I want my car to run without repairs. I want to be famous and wealthy. I want my law practice to thrive, a miraculous flower. I want to live forever. I want to be a champion figure skater, or ski jumper.

I want *everything*, and I want to pay for none of it.

My car is an old Mazda. My house a late fifties ranch. I live in the suburbs with my wife. I love her, I really do.

Sometimes the sink doesn't drain. This morning the cat turds got stuck in the toilet and I had to use a plunger to get it working. The roof leaks. The elbow under the kitchen sink is rotting through and we have a bucket under it. I have promised to fix the leak. For some reason, I can't bring myself to do it.

My voice, to my dismay, has come to sound like my father's. My father, an engineer, spent his whole life at Westinghouse making vacuum tubes. My mother, she spent a good portion of hers not being there because of it. A race was on. Unprecedented strides were being made in solid-state circuitry. My father's division worked overtime, and then some, trying to catch up.

A vacuum, he would say, over breakfast, and that's what he'd get from my mother.

It was her form of protest.

You listening, Curtis? he'd ask.

From the time I was seven I knew the laws of thermodynamics. My father taught them to me:

1) Energy is neither created nor destroyed.

2) All systems tend toward disorder unless acted upon.

He even had a snappy little equation for me: $dS = dQ/T$ —*where dS is an infinitesimal change in the measure for a system absorbing an infinitesimal quantity of heat dQ at absolute temperature T.*

I forget the remainder. This was enough for a boy of eight to think about. Why does a rocket work in space, Curtis? my father would ask. Any untroubled boy's response to that question would be like mine had been: because it pushes off. The flame and stuff coming out the bottom makes it go. No, my father corrected. What is there to push off from in space? It's a vacuum.

I never argued with him about vacuums. He was an expert there.

Nolo contendere, Pops.

But I thought about them, how in science fiction movies if you were thrown out into space your face swelled and exploded.

Eat your cereal, my father said.

Now, still, I imagine celery, chicken, peaches, coming apart inside me. Everything is coming apart. It was all coming together, and now, looking off into the not too distant future, things are coming apart.

Your birthday is next week, my wife, Beth, tells me at breakfast. Do you have any idea of what you want to do?

I smile.

I imagine hang gliding over the beach nearby. Or racing up Highway 101 on an expensive Italian motorcycle. I'll fly to Zanzibar, or Morocco. *I think this is the beginning of a beautiful relationship*, etc. etc.

I am swimming among the biscuits in my cereal bowl.

The idea of cake depresses me. The prospect of a binge drunk is no better.

The cereal box reads, *New! New! New! Now Crunchier, Toastier, Tastier!*

Curtis, Beth says, but I am far away.

.

I make great efforts. I am not a failure.

I have a handful of degrees, undergraduate and graduate, have worked at twenty or so jobs, most of them professional. I have won trophies, much in the way my father did, for his vacuum tubes. Each one gave me a little jolt and I was pushed forward. Focus was everything.

Years went by in a flash. Was I happy? I have no way of knowing.

.

So I'm at the DQ. There's a guy that slides around the back of my car and lifts the lid off the dumpster. He's got a hot dog there, and half a chocolate malt.

Free.

When he leaves I am compelled to lift the lid and look inside.

Whatever it is, I won't eat it, I promise myself.

.

Life is expensive, a friend told me.

She'd bought a painting that day. We were both poor, and she'd paid three hundred some dollars for the painting. This was nearly a decade ago.

I got a vicarious thrill, a stab of joy at seeing her stand beside the painting. My wife does not like to hear about this woman. I loved her too, this other, earlier one. But that is over.

.

Think, I think.

Beth and I lie side by side. We do not make love as frequently as we once did. Or as insanely. She wants me to brush my teeth first. She doesn't like the stubble on my chin. We do things slowly. She tells me she's changed for me. She says this as if I haven't for her. Now, though, we are sometimes tired. Sometimes sick with the world. I want to jump up and scream for joy, toss it all off! Why don't I?

It's the car, Beth says. It's making that noise again.

What noise? I ask.

You know, the one that sounds like one of those electric grilling machines. I ask her to imitate the sound for me. I already know this sound. It's the oil pump, which might, or might not, conk out and ruin the whole engine—maybe even with Beth in the car, driving to or from work morning or evening, in the dark. My mechanic tells me, Don't worry. The oil light will come on first.

Then what? I ask.

Stop the car, he says.

Right.

I'm at the K-Mart not far from my home. They've tossed all kinds of broken toys in the dumpsters. I dig through them, in my tie and suit coat. I've parked the Mazda off a ways.

A clerk comes out the back door.

Can I help you, sir? he says. He eyes me with great suspicion. I am a living, breathing anomaly. A snag in the fabric.

Lawyers do not dig in dumpsters behind the local K-Mart.

Destitute crazies don't wear Brooks Brothers three-piece pin-striped suits and silk ties.

Hey! the clerk says.

I will not be embarrassed. Will not blush. Will not turn from him, as I did, when Cindy Palco, the most desired girl in my junior high class, decided she wanted me. She couldn't have me. I wasn't fit. Her breasts were too large and I wanted her too badly. My face gave me away.

I wasn't ready.

Don't bug me, I tell the clerk, and he turns on his heel and is through the back door quicker than I can think *Police*.

.

Suddenly I hate litigation. Especially insurance litigation, which is what I do, for Smith and Ziegler. Cars, I know, carom off one another like ball bearings in a coffee can.

Smaller can, or more ball bearings—more collisions.

Outside forces, acting upon the system, may also increase collisions. Read: God, the cat, grandmother, a sticky accelerator pedal, boys on bridges with bricks, fatigue, etc.

I would like to act upon a good number of my clients, with their phony aches and pains, their trumped up indignities and falsified truths.

Here, I say, and hand one a week old donut I've scrounged from the Lindquist Bakery dumpster on the way to work. Have a doughnut. They're free.

The real cases, they break my heart.

Accidents, it seems, are inevitable.

.

Are you all right? Beth asks. It is Thursday. I have three days. Three days to read the *Koran, Anna Karenina,* and *Gravity's Rainbow.* Three days to travel to Tahiti, write a bestseller, and take up hot air ballooning. Three days to have an affair with the woman of my dreams, three days to end it, three days to decide not to have it in the first place, three days to have the children we don't have, three days three days three days.

And on the third day, he—

What?

We are drinking coffee in the rumpus room.

Any resolutions? Beth asks.

Don't remind me, I say. She means my birthday. I have not told her about my stealing.

Beth snuggles up beside me on the couch. Come on, she says. You can tell me. What do you really want for your birthday?

I'm stumped.

I picture sloops under full sail, sandy beaches, young bodies. The hard crack of a bat, ball flying high and into the bleachers, a homer. Running effortlessly, joyfully! Spray of ruby-red grapefruit. Buxom starlet in aquamarine décolletage dress.

I hunger.

Tell me, she teases.

I am speechless, torn.

I remind myself of a robot in an old science fiction movie, "Forbidden Planet."

Robby, aim at the captain's head and fire, Dr. Morbius says, in a now famous scene. The captain and crew of the visiting spaceship stare, dumbstruck. The robot takes aim and is suddenly engulfed in electrical flame. The captain and crew are visibly relieved. Dr. Morbius chuckles. Robby cannot override the prime directive, he explains, to protect human life. Ordering him to fire at you.... Well, you can see. If I left him like this he would burn out every circuit in his body.

I smile a reassuring smile, myself again.

Beth is lovely.

Come on, she says. You've got to be able to come up with something.

She is wearing a shirt with a button-down front, a saucy wedge of cleavage there. She grins.

Come on, off the top of your head!

All right, I say. Since you wanted me to start there, how about if I grew my hair back?

Stop being so silly, she says, and ruffles what remains. Don't be a spoil-sport.

.

At the dry cleaners, I palm half a pack of paper clips.

At the mechanic's, a handful of pens: *Jerry's Automotive Specialties*, the pens read. I tell myself I'm helping him advertise. I'll leave them on my desk where my clients will steal them.

There is a way to twist bottles from a pop machine at the marina where we go sailing summers and I'm tempted to drive there on the way home from work.

An invisible hand tugs at the wheel. It is all I can do to stay on the highway.

I break out in a sweat. My heart pounds.

.

Forty years ago, I'm a blip on an oscilloscope. A backfire. A cosmic accident. My mother's body yawns wide and here I am.

I think this at the dinner table, the cake in front of me, candles lit:

Time, that's what I'm stealing.

I look around the table. It is a quiet moment, faces aglow.

Make a wish! my Uncle Lou tells me.

Everyone smiles.

I am reminded of countless birthdays, Christmas dinners, Thanksgiving Day meals, send offs and returns and just get-togethers. Time trails behind us like a sloughed off skin.

It occurs to me how much we are all a part of each other.

Even my father, ten years gone.

Not vacuum.

Yeah, come on, Curtis, my aunt Myrna says. And besides, she adds, the fatal forties don't last forever.

None of it does! my mother laughs.

Beth squeezes my arm. I take a quick breath, and hold it, bent over the cake.

I wish—

A great, cavernous hollow yawns inside me.

You can't say what the wish is or it won't come true, Uncle Lou teases.

I press my eyes shut—

Heat of the candles on my forehead. Lou clearing his throat. Beth's perfume, a rose scent.

Just a little longer, I wish, silently, then blow the room dark.

3

Those People

Eighty Acres

It was just me and my brother Paul at the coops when Hondo come home with his new truck, ready to kill. He'd been down at Rose's, drinking hard, and as he lurched across the lawn I stepped out in front of him like a fool. You see, me and Paul, we're looking out for old Hondo.

"Where you goin'?" I says, and Hondo fakes to the right, but Paul's there, and then to the left, but I'm way ahead of him. Which was crazy, because then Hondo had nowhere to go but right through me, which he did, putting his knee in my stomach first. And Hondo is *big*—six six or something, and built like a bull's backside.

"I'm gonna kill that son-of-a-bitch sold me that truck," he says, "and that no-good wife of mine."

I was bent over, holding my gut. Paul had me under the arm. Hondo goes through his door, two down from mine, and I seen there eighty acres and a whole life with it disappearing, like Hondo's shoulders into the dark.

"We gotta do something," I says to Paul.

"What?" Paul says.

Paul's one of those skinny guys, got no meat on his bones—a lightweight, and he's been sick, too. Me, I'm right in the middle. Paul looks at me and I look right back. Hondo's rummaging around in his room for his rifle, busting everything up in the process, real noisy. Dark in there, since he knocked out all the lights.

"You just stand here," I says to Paul, and he does, out front of Hondo's door, his eyes all screwed up and worried.

There's a maple tree, whirligigs in the grass, and Paul starts picking through for ones that'll fly, easing down toward the gate out to the street. It's a ruse, and I can see he's figuring to bolt.

"Don't move," I says to Paul.

And all the while, Hondo's banging off his walls, and we're hoping maybe, like most times, that'll be it. But no, here comes Hondo right out his door with his rifle, and me, all of a sudden I'm on my hands and knees up beside the coops, thick grass and them bitter-sweet smelling dandelions everywhere. I don't even know what I'm looking for, when I've got my hands on it, a two-by-four with a sheet of plastic stapled on top to cover the mower we pawned a few months back.

"Out of the way, Paul," Hondo says. He's swaying like a badly built bridge in a wind storm and what does Paul do but start laughing.

Hondo's got a real temper, and right there, his face goes all red. Three strikes and you're out. That rip-off truck, Rose asking for a divorce, and Paul, laughing, is just enough to put Hondo over the edge, and he raises his rifle a little, and it makes it all the easier for me to do what I had in mind to do—hit a home run, Hondo's head being the ball. It made a sound like thwoking a big watermelon at the A & P, and Hondo went right over into all them dandelions, face first. Paul stood staring, his mouth open like a trap door.

"Shut it, Paul," I says, and he did, and we turned old Hondo over and made sure he was comfortable.

Dusk was coming on, the sky the color of a peach. It would have been nice sitting alongside old Hondo, but we were in trouble now, and had to act quick. We'd been waiting, hoping things would straighten out of themselves. Now, Old Mrs. Kern, from up the hill, would be over, and what were we going to do then? I gave it some thought, and with that sunset and all, I got sidetracked. Me and Paul and Hondo, I was thinking.

We'd all come to the coops together after Calmenson Paper laid us off. Cheapest rent around: rooms, sort of, in a cleaned up chicken coop downwind from the old house. An outbuilding, that's what it was, on a farm, the town built up around on all sides but the west. There, eighty acres of prime dirt stretched just about as far as the eye could see, and every last one Old Lady Kern's. People had been lusting after that land for some time. Old Lady Kern, they said, she's gotta go sooner or later.

I looked west. Now I lusted, too. Rolling hills, all in clover, a river running through it, a couple high spots, brown-tipped, like nipples. I had a desire to run a plow up those old hills. Plant a few acres of corn. On the east, I'd put up a cabin, some elms and maples, and down by the river, birch. It was like a vision, that cabin, smoke curling out the chimney and those trees, leaves fluttering in the breeze and sounding like running water.

I ached for it, is what I'm saying.

.

"Ruben," Paul says. "What're we gonna do?"

I reeled myself back in. We had to act fast.

"Gimme a second," I said.

The sky had gone a shade darker. We'd have to get Hondo in soon for his big performance. The thought of it made me sick. Only, we did have one thing going for us: Mrs. Kern didn't come down nights until Hondo's lights went on. And that gave me cause to chuckle.

Old Hondo'd found Jesus a few months back, and lost his wife in the process. "I am the way and the light,' he'd bellowed the week after his baptism. He looked pretty funny, his gut hanging out, preaching off that elm stump. "You heathens," he said—and he being Chippewa like Paul and me, all raised Mediwiwin, his saying it came as something of a shock—"Repent and lay down in the Life of the Lord."

I reached under Hondo's head and felt for the bump. He had a good-sized one; I hadn't wanted to hit him and not knock him out.

"Help me pull him into his room," I said.

As I'd suspected, Paul, sick as he was, was no help at all. You have no idea how heavy a body is until you try to move one—you see it all the time in murder mysteries and what not and they just whisk the thing away. But no, Hondo, since he'd been going to all those church meetings, basement pot-lucks, and devotional pizzas, had put on some weight.

"Jesus," Paul said. His face turned lavender and we hadn't even got Hondo halfway to his door.

"You can say that again," I said.

I had Hondo under the arms, and thought I might herniate myself, trying to lift him like that, so I got down on the other end with Paul, and we pulled on those fancy boots of his, Red Wings, and he slid right across the grass there so nice we forgot to slow down and his head made that melon sound again when we pulled him over the stoop and into his room.

"Oops," Paul said.

I checked to see Hondo was still breathing. Got down on my hands and knees. Breath you wouldn't believe.

"Okay," I says.

Paul just stands there, his hands hanging at his sides like they do. He's a little lacking in the mental department, see. Mercury, from up at Calmenson Paper done it, only nobody listens. Methyl mercury. He was mixing paper in vats with a thing like a canoe paddle, steam coming right up in his face. Mercury? How? they said. But who listens to a half-blood Chippewa? It's drink that done it, they said.

"Put your hands in your pockets," I says.

But now Paul's got the shakes coming on. I might have to knock him down and get his tongue out of his throat. All that exercise's set him off and there go his eyes, rolling back and goddamn if Mrs. Kern isn't lookin' out her kitchen window, just waiting.

It's dark in Hondo's room, and I can't see. I gotta get something to pull Paul's tongue out.

"Jesus!" I say to myself, and Hondo grunts.

But here come Paul's eyes, focusing on me, and he's going to be all right.

"Siddown," I say, taking Paul's shoulder.

.

So we sit, the three of us in the dark there. Hondo, on the floor, his back up against the stove, Paul in one ladder-back chair and me in another, waiting for Paul's breathing to even out. It's just too much, I think; and then I pinch my thigh—real hard. Two big sins, if you ask me: self-pitying, and not giving the other guy a fair shake. So I stop the one and do the other. Still, it's complicated and makes no sense.

There at Calmenson Paper, Paul starts shaking and having fits and his eyes roll back in his head. I go in to talk to the big cheese, Earl Carter, bring Paul with me, and Hondo for support. Hondo's got his Bible tucked under his arm, is in that reading verses over lunch phase (one I went through years back myself).

"Your job there's poisoning my brother," I says. "Lookit him. He's ruined already."

Paul was in-between fits.

Earl bridged his arms out on his desk. There was a fluorescent light and it buzzed. The office smelled of coffee. I was thirsty. Earl shook his head.

"Ruben," he says, "I'm sick and tired of you Indians coming to work drunk and cryin' sick. You hear me?"

I said I did. I also said this wasn't drinking.

"It's like something I saw in a magazine," I says. "Happened to a whole lot of Japanese people got poisoned with mercury."

Earl's look got uglier. Right away I seen that went over real good with him, what I'd just said. Earl had been in the Big War, in the Pacific.

I was stumped.

And then, right then, as if we'd timed it or something, Paul's eyes roll back in his head and he goes all spastic, flops down on Earl's desk, coffee mug and papers flying. He's going there like a windmill in a hurricane until Hondo gets his arms around his waist and squeezes, and I go after his tongue. In a minute it's all over.

But Earl, he's pissed.

"Get that... *garbage* out of my office," he says. "All of you—"

And that's when I gave him my armed services best, a fistful of U. S. of A. right in the mouth. Fired, all three of us. Right there, complete with police escort and a night in jail for me. Later, I called about severance pay. Earl said we'd have to sue to collect. So we were out on our asses and broke, Paul sick, and Hondo with that new truck of his, sitting all shiny out front, the sun glaring off the hood so bad mornings we could hardly bear to drive it.

In the unemployment office, Paul's okay, but as soon as we're looking for work, sure enough, he gets to breathing hard for nervousness, and there he goes, along with whatever job we'd wanted. All shot to hell. And like in that old hand basket, away we go, right down the ladder, one rung at a time, and end up living in these outbuildings, dirt floor and all—I mean, we'd really hit bottom. And as a last slap in the face, the cowboy who sold Hondo the truck didn't mention the sawdust he put in the crankcase so the rods wouldn't rattle and now they do. That engine sounds like a bunch of spray cans with those beads in the bottom all shaking. A real case of terminal rod-knock. Seventeen hundred bucks worth of truck up in smoke, and half of mine.

That's what I was thinking, sitting there in the dark. That, and I was saying a little prayer. Don't mistake me. I'm no believer in visions and voices, and I'm no saint. But something in me won't let go of that, and right there, I got to mumbling to myself, couldn't even think what to say.

I stood, looked at my chair, sitting empty. And out of nowhere, I think—*that's it!*

I went down to my room at the end of the coops, got two bulbs, come back and put them in Hondo's sockets, but didn't turn them on. It was pitch black, the sun gone down, and the crickets chirring.

"Paul," I says. "Help me get ol' Hondo here up into this chair."

We were short on time and I rushed things. I hoped Paul didn't have another seizure. His face was still a little blue. We got Hondo into the chair, and I held him by the shoulder.

"You hold him now Paul," I said, and went out to Hondo's truck for the tow rope.

I wrapped that bristly rope around Hondo three or four times. Set the other chair across from him. Put out the checkers and board. That rope pulling around his middle must have done it, because he had to get sick, right on the table and everything. Then it was into the shower for Lysol, scrubbing the board and the table clean. I was desperate. Everything we were working towards, hoping for, would be done and gone if Old Mrs. Kern so much as caught a whiff of Hondo's breath. So I just tilted Hondo's head back and gargled him a bit with that Lysol. It must have burned something awful, because ol' Hondo sat right up, his eyes wide. He flapped his arms at his sides and started shouting.

"Jee-sus Kee-riste!" he shouts.

And just as quick he slumps over again.

I pulled back one of Hondo's curtains. Old Mrs. Kern was still waiting there, though by the door now. The moon was coming out, and the room was flooded with silver light. The place smelled like a hospital.

"Paul," I said, "go back to your room," but he shakes his head no. "Go on," I says.

But Paul won't budge. He gets scared when he has seizures, and I can't blame him. He gets this bright look on his face, slips into Hondo's bed, pulls the covers up under his chin, smiles that ruined smile of his, and I think, what the hell.

I set a stool behind Hondo, made sure I could fit between him and the wall, and reached for the light switch.

.

She took her time getting down to the coops, I can tell you that much. Hondo settled into his chair, and then he reached back and ran his fingers up and down my scalp and mumbled Annabelle, oh Annabelle and Patty, and Susan, none of which was the name of his wife. I pinched him, and he just grinned and started all over again.

Until I used the corkscrew in my jackknife. Finally, there was the rattle of Mrs. Kern at the door, and I said, as deeply and slowly as I could, "Come-mon nin," imitating Hondo's drawl.

The bulbs I'd gotten from my unit were forties, and between the room being dim, and Mrs. Kern's already bad eyes, cataracts like marbles under bottle bottom lenses, she had to feel her way to sit. She squeezed between the chair and table, round as an apple, smiled, dumplings under her chin. I noticed she'd forgotten to shave her moustache.

"Oh-kay?" she says, adjusting her hearing aid. There's a big dial on the front, like on a radio, and she turns it this way and that, then messes with her necklace. "You vant you should start?"

I grunted affirmation, and reached out from behind Hondo and moved my first checker. Tonight Hondo was red.

"Zo," she says, countering my move, "I tell you a-bout hahs-bahnd in old country."

I don't know what kind of checker player Hondo was, but Mrs. Kern was shrewd. And she cheated, and to make things worse, as I've already shown, I've got a mean temper, and am a poor loser. I hate to lose so much I usually don't play at all. Pride, I suppose. They were unable to beat it out of me at that reservation school. I'm a big sinner in that category.

So there I am. I turn my head a second to check on Paul, and what does Old Lady Kern do but snap on a king, just a flash out of the corner of my eye. And when I'm looking at her again, she sits, back straight, all quiet and honest. And she is, I suppose, but for checkers.

"Vell, Homer," she says.

Homer? We hadn't called Hondo that since we were kids and playing baseball and he'd knocked one ball after another into the creek past the outfield.

"Yah?" I says, pulling on Hondo's braids so his head nods, and she just launches right back in.

Checkers. I was giving her a run for her money, but I got the feeling, from the sour look on her face, that I'd better just go ahead and let her wipe the board with me. Only, somehow, I couldn't.

"I zee playing you vell too-night," Mrs. Kern said.

I raised Hondo's right hand, a gesture of humility. I was thinking proud thoughts.

And then she kinged me.

Cheater.

.

I wanted that game over. Then the next, and the one after that. She told me about her daughter, Liza, and her son, Cojneck, and her three husbands. Coal miners, each dead of black lung before thirty, her son and daughter killed in the war.

"It vas good ting I marry young," she said. "I caught them up to. Quick," she said, holding up her index finger. "And den, Valter," she said.

She shook her head, put a palm to her cheek, and those big old blinded up eyes of hers got all the more rheumy looking. I thought she might cry. Out of the blue, Hondo stirred. He reached for my hair.

"Patty," he said, "Oh, Patty."

I got my hands around his throat, tried to cut him back a bit.

"Vhat?" Mrs. Kern said. "Vhat?"

"Pretty," I said. "*Pret-tee.*"

Mrs. Kern fingered her necklace. About two pounds of fake pearls. "*Bee*-u-tee-ful," she says, proudly. "All real lan-atic pearl. From Valter."

Her eyes behind those bottle bottom lenses got all glassy again. I just let her sit.

.

I was in pain, waiting. My guts rumbled, not having eaten well lately, and the stool was hard and cold, a metal one Hondo'd taken from Calmenson Paper the day we'd been fired. Looking around, I could see his whole place was furnished in Calmenson Modern: metal bookshelves, file cases with a door over, the table, curtains with ocean liners sailing proudly across.

Paul turned in Hondo's bed. I reached into my pocket and rubbed my cedarbark charm. I wondered, as I sometimes did, if maybe the two things, this prayerin', and the charms I made, didn't work against each other and maybe I should go with just one or the other. And all the while, Old Mrs. Kern is way inside herself across the table, tears in her eyes. I could cry, too, I think, angry like, and right there I get this impulse to slap Old Mrs. Kern alongside the head, but where it really comes from is jealousy.

You see, I *can't* cry. And what good would it do if I did? I was thinking, sitting there mad enough to spit tacks. Would it help me with Paul? Put bread on the table? Get me a pair of shoes? Would it fix what's happened, or give us Indians our land back? And somehow it always comes to that last thing, so while Old Mrs. Kern is indulging herself, I think about it:

Land.

It's like air to us Chippewa. Only, we lost ours. All parceled out on paper, in a language with lots of *wheretofors* and what not, such that most whites don't even understand it. A bunch of them bought farms on Chippewa reserves not knowing any better, or not caring. Threw up barns and outbuildings like so many mushrooms. Walter Kern was one of them: stole his farm with a bottle of whiskey and a few blankets.

I'd heard about it from my mother: *Chingus!* she spat, weasel. Living there, I'd given it some thought.

So when Hondo told me Old Mrs. Kern was talking putting him on permanent—and that's the word she used, *permanent*—I was all ears. Tell me more, I said, and he did.

"She's talkin' about writing me into her will," he said, and while he talked on, I had that dream:

The cabin with the smoke curling out, Paul on a brick-red tractor, puttering along. We could handle that. Corn. Eighty acres, blowin' in the breeze, and in June, lightning bugs, blinking all over it.

"She catches me drinkin' though," Hondo said, "and she won't consider it. Says I got to prove myself. 'I got Jesus,' I told her."

God help us all, I thought.

The table shook, and I startled.

"Your move," Old Mrs. Kern says.

I'd forgotten about the board. There were more kings now than we had playing pieces; which is to say, she'd brought a few of her own. They weren't even the same black exactly. More of a deep charcoal, but she'd gotten them underneath.

So what to do?

I had to think, Old Mrs. Kern sitting across the table. She wouldn't want a dummy running her farm, or a hot head, or somebody who'd fight with her, I knew that. And the funny thing was, Hondo, if he'd been losing bad as I was, he'd've thrown the board, sent the pieces over hell and back. Or, he'd've punched somebody.

"Gimme a second," I says in a gruff voice.

I just couldn't figure it. I'd peeked through the window one night, both of them there at the table looking gloomy. Hondo reaches across the checkers and puts his hand on Old Mrs. Kern's forearm, and she busted down and cried.

"Valter," she says, and Hondo'd replied, "We all got to lose things sometimes."

Now I looked at her across the table, straight on. She blinked behind those glasses, her eyes more like porpoises's eyes I seen at the zoo in St. Paul, set way in there and shining blind like aluminum foil. She had on this old gingham dress, washed to rags. She looked pretty tired. I thought about my mother, Papagine, and how big she'd got there at the end. Bad diet, lots of salt pork and white flour. Something shook in me and I swallowed, something not quite bitter, but to my taste pretty awful. I choked it down.

"All right," I says. "You win."

And right there, Old Mrs. Kern's head hit the table. Fallen dead asleep. Broke the dial on her hearing aid, and when she roused, me pulling from behind, she set up a shouting at first, until she felt for that box on her chest and seen it was broken.

"Broke," I said. "*Broke!*"

I shut off the lights, stood holding her in the dark, then thought just to put her in Hondo's bed. After all, he was still sagged over in his chair, roped in. So I half-drag, half-guide her over into the corner and set her down. I pull back the blanket, and get a fistful of blood hammering in my head. But Old Mrs. Kern's already swinging her legs in and there's no turning back.

"Mrs. Kern," I says, and getting nothing in return, I think she's out. Both of them.

I went back to the table, and in the dark, swept the board and checkers into the box. It's real quiet there, and all of a sudden I realize Paul's quit snoring.

"Oh.... Oh my," Old Mrs. Kern says, "Oh.... My.... goodness!"

I slipped out the door and sat on that elm stump, the sky clear and inviting and dark; it just went on and on. Paul had always been a shy one, and hadn't ever had any luck with girls.

.

Some time later, Old Mrs. Kern slipped out the door and went up the hill to her house. I couldn't tell whether it was a spring in her step, or anger that propelled her. She didn't stop by Hondo's the night after, or the night after that, but when she did, she came with a short, pock-faced man wearing a dark suit and hat. *John Law*, I thought, watching them cross the yard and go into Hondo's unit.

I worried. I could just taste that cellblock.

I'd told Paul the day after he'd been with a girl he'd had his eye on, Evelynn Jackson. It didn't matter that neither of us had seen Evelynn in over a year. Paul was that addled.

I paced.

I'd take responsibility myself, I thought, if it came to that; but could Hondo take care of Paul? I doubted it. Time crawled by. Paul was scared too, just watching me, and had one of his fits. I knocked him down and lay on top of him so he wouldn't hurt himself. His tongue got way back down his throat, and I had to use the handle of my spatula to get him breathing. We got all messed up there.

"Okay, buddy?" I said when he'd calmed down.

He nodded and slid up against my bed. Somebody knocked on the door, and for a second, I couldn't force myself up to open it. I says a little prayer and stood.

"Ruben," Hondo says, "open the goddamned door. I got somethin' to show ya."

I threw back the bolt. Hondo stepped in beaming from ear to ear.

"It's a goddamned miracle," he says, shaking a sheaf of papers.

I dropped down to that dirt floor.

"Ruben," Hondo says, shaking me. "Ruben!"

But I can't see to stand, digging and filling my mouth, and won't be distracted.

Monster

Its tail a dash of neon fire, the Monster makes its final descent, children screaming. Myron Little, his hand on the brake, pulls back, the cars roaring past him, rattling. Halfway into the first climb, the Monster slows, stops, then rolls back to the platform where Myron stands, dreading the moment he will have to turn now, yet again, and take on new passengers.

"Everybody out!" he hollers.

Children pour from the Monster's back, shouting, laughing, boasting. One small boy staggers, his balance affected. Myron gets his arm around the boy's shoulder, steadying him.

"Come on, Champ," he says, fatherly.

Heart pounding, Myron looks down into the crowd for the boy's parents—one mass of expectant faces—and for Aja. Aja Dibikamig, who he hasn't seen in years. Aja, who he still thinks of as his *niinimoshen*, his sweetheart.

"Tough it out there," Myron tells the boy, but he doesn't feel too tough himself right now.

Usually, when the carnival wins the bid on the Forest Lake show, he opts out for the weekend. But this time he is broke; and he is something else now, after all these years—something he can't quite explain to himself: *ready*.

Myron ushers the boy through the gate and a woman with stiff, platinum hair takes him by the hand.

"Thank you," she says.

Myron counts heads. Girls in tank tops and platform sandals, teenaged boys with pork chop sideburns and wispy moustaches, parents with children. He smells apple perfume, and buttery popcorn, and on the breeze coming up from the lake, where the bikers have parked, marijuana.

Myron smiles, and taking a deep breath, begins:

Step right up and ride the Monster! He reaches for the mike. His voice crackles. *The one and only Monster straight out of Red Lake County, the one and only of its kind. See the glowing eyes, the scaly body, the fiery tail! She jumps, she flies, she goes under water. It's all in a ride on the Monster. See the cavern dwelling vampires, the gargoyles of the Moon. Watch the creeping skeletons in the graveyard and all of it from the Monster. Step right up, it's worth the price and more!*

Myron unhooks the gate chain and the children filter through.

Four tickets please. Four tickets. See the Monster. Ride the monster.

Twenty-five, twenty-six, twenty-seven....

It's a thrill, it's a chill, it's like nothing you've ever experienced!

Thirty.

"All right," he says.

A small boy tries to squeeze by and Myron forces him back. Narrow shoulders, nearly double-lidded eyes, dark hair and high cheekbones. The boy grips the gate and stares. He looks a bit like Aja, and Myron is surprised to find himself blinking. He feels sick to his stomach, can't take his eyes off the kid.

Is it possible?

"You're up next," Myron says, and winks.

The boy's eyes drilling into him from behind, Myron works the Monster. Pulls a lever that drops a mechanical spider, another that makes three skeletons tap dance, a third that causes a plume of flame to leap from a crater. The ride lasts just a little over fourteen minutes, but now, this time around, it seems to take forever. From time to time

Myron glances over his shoulder. The boy does not take his eyes from him, not for a second. Myron shudders. He feels a kind of dread settle over him. He counts: the Monster in the Magic Mountain—fifteen, sixteen, seventeen... Pushes the button for the steam. And out again, dizzying, green and red and blue lights. Sparks fly from the castors. Grease turns liquid and puffs from under the cars. The big electric motor in the platform hums, smells like lightning. Then, around a sharp curve, and Splash! The monster drops down into water, snakes into the Tunnel of Love. There are squeals of laughter. A boy's voice: "Oh Yuck! He's kissin' her," and another, deeper voice: "I'm gonna kill you if you don't shut up, you little prick."

Myron checks his watch. He pushes a red button on the side: Four and a half minutes. He kicks his boot into the control stand, distracted. The boy's face rises up everywhere, Aja's.

.

On a night like this, seven years ago, he'd picked Aja up after her shift at the Old Fashioned Popcorn Stand. They were working the carnival circuit to get away from school—he'd been on the GI bill, Aja had been putting herself through. That night, he'd done something he shouldn't have, and was afraid it showed. He'd driven the car with a certain over-caution uncharacteristic of him, feigning a carefree indifference, his hand hung over the wheel.

"A little hot, isn't it?" Aja asked.

"Is it?" Myron replied.

He'd stopped alongside the road and pulled the top down. It was a cool, July evening. His heart was pounding and he'd broken out in a sweat. When he was back in the car, Aja ran her fingers up his neck. This was something Myron usually liked.

"Have a nice night?" she asked.

"No," Myron said, flinching, pulling back into the road. Aja ran her fingers over his scalp. His scalp prickled.

"How about tonight?" she asked.

"What?"

"You know what." She twirled a shock of his hair around a finger and tugged on it. Hard. It hurt.

"Cut it out," Myron said.

He'd glanced over at her. The wind tossed back her hair. Her breasts strained the material of her bodice; her hips were full and curvy; her legs long. She looked, in moonlight, beautiful and cruel.

"Aw, Jesus," he'd said.

.

Which is what he says now, an attractive couple pressing at the gate, the girl laughing, long-haired and pretty, the kid putting on a show of toughness, dark-eyed and hungry, the boy peering out from behind them. Aw, Jesus. He doesn't need this. He doesn't need this at all. He feels something tug at him right down to his toes, a kind of emptiness, one he feels himself falling into, a scary, weightless turning end over end.

Myron grips the brake lever.

He will not look at the boy, will not, he promises himself, counting, but at that very second, his eyes find the boy's, and they lock there.

Thirty-five, thirty-six.

The kid looks just like Aja, he thinks, and forces himself to turn away. But Aja's face, now, is everywhere, and nowhere.

.

How he'd loved her!

He'd met her a party in the Twin Cities, just back from Vietnam and acting crazy; Aja was out of school and running from the reserve. He'd mistaken her for a white girl, and had said something awful. What's your real name? she'd asked him. Timber Nigger, he'd said.

Later, at a powwow up at White Earth, he'd seen her again, and knew her for the mixed blood she was.

Myron had been mortified.

She'd had a number of dancers courting and Myron could only admire her from a distance. She was beautiful and much sought after. Myron's costume was makeshift, dyed turkey feathers instead of eagle, horse hair instead of porcupine quill—and he had no trailer, as did the other, better dancers. Still, when he'd looked at her, his insides turned to mush.

All that night, he tried to bolster himself to so much as say hello. There was fighting, boasting, posturing around her. Myron, thinking he couldn't stand a minute more, stepped out into the open from behind a Satellite and crossed the tented field to his aunt's fry bread stand.

"Gimme four, Gert," he said to the woman behind the counter. He was too fat already, but only fry bread could satisfy him. He thought of it as comfort food.

Gert was back in seconds, four stuffed napkins transparent with oil, fry bread wrapped inside. Myron's mouth watered. He took a large bite of the first.

"Havin' a nice night?" Gert asked.

"Jesus Chrise," he said.

He was suddenly happy. He started in on the second, and when someone stood to his right, he turned to see who it was, grinning like a fool.

"You got enough for me?" the girl said, something coiled and teasing in her voice.

He tried to swallow. She smiled, her dark eyes aglitter. He tried to say something, then held out a napkin and fry bread, it was the only thing he could think to do. She turned the napkin back and slowly bit down, her teeth pearly white. The gesture made something go loose in his middle.

"So, how's dancing?"

"Shitty," he managed to say. "Danced real shitty."

Aja smiled. "Like your moccasins."

Myron had no moccasins, and so had cut the tops off a pair of boots. There was a hole in the front of the left, and his toe was sticking through.

Myron could only laugh.

They talked for some time, he kind of babbling, Aja firing questions at him as though they'd never had that awful interaction earlier. The other dancers, thinking she'd left them to find a port-a-potty, spied her with Myron and headed over.

"You have a car?" she asked.

"You bet," Myron said.

.

Accidents. Good ones and bad. That was life.

That night, he'd thought the drive would amount to nothing. He put the top down. He loved the car, an Oldsmobile with chrome bumpers up front like tits: *Dagmars* they called them back then. But now it seemed horrendous, embarrassing. The seats were torn and patched with duct tape, the steering wheel broken and epoxied. The windshield was cracked and the radio didn't work. He had two horses, and had thrown the saddles in back before he'd driven down for powwow—the saddles and the car were the only things in the world he had that were worth anything—and now he noticed the saddles smelled. *Stunk really.* Well, he thought, they weren't worth much either. Nothing was.

Now, at the wheel, seeing the car through Aja's eyes, the car looked like a cruel joke. After all, what did he have to show for himself? He was a basket-case, nearly jumped out of his skin if he heard a car backfire, or a door slap shut, and only that through sheer force of will.

Aja held her head out the window. He was astounded at her beauty. She had a scar running the length of her cheek, and her nose was a little crooked, but somehow that just made things worse: It made her real.

Somehow, his defects did not work the same magic, he thought. He was big around the gut, his chin not big or square enough. He hadn't shaved, and he hadn't showered after dancing. He thought to button his vest over his belly, but what was the use?

Aja's hair caught in the breeze. It tossed and fell over her back, coiling on itself and shimmering, dark as molasses.

"You're different," she said.

Myron didn't know whether to laugh or cry. He couldn't think of anything to say. Yes, he was *different* all right. He was wound tight as a spring. Try as he might, he just couldn't let go.

"I like to drive," he said.

He found himself grinning. Well, at least that was true. One time he'd told a woman he was a helicopter

pilot—which he hadn't been. He'd been a PFC, a grunt, a shooter. He'd had a very hard time talking himself out of that one.

"Lucielle, here—she's all right."

He patted the tape beside him, and to his horror Aja slid over.

"You want to turn around?" he asked.

"No," she said.

Even her name roused him: Aja, *Carried Across*. And Dibikamig? *Big hearted.* He tried to think of something flashy to say. Something that would win her. He felt a yearning inside, a hollow. In the end he could think of nothing, so said,

"Tell me about yourself."

And to his surprise, she did. She told him about going to school out east, her small apartment, and the cockroaches. About her roommates, Cheryl and Lisa. About her strange brother, who was building TVs.

She said she didn't like the forty-niners, the parties after powwow, or the dancers that wouldn't leave her alone. Myron nodded.

"Terrible," he said. "Just terrible."

She didn't know what she wanted. She was going to be twenty-three in a few days. She wanted to go back to the university out east, to graduate school. What did he think of that?

"What do you want to study?" Myron asked.

"Most everybody else asks what I want to go for. I mean, why graduate school?"

"Well?"

"I don't know."

She asked him if he knew what he wanted, if he had plans.

"I'm keeping my options open," he told her. "There's a whole world out there." He felt like an ass saying it. Jesus, Myron, he thought. Completely! "I'd like to travel," he said. He couldn't stop himself, Oh, what a man of the world he was now! he thought.

But under it all, he knew exactly what he wanted. He wanted to say: What I want is you, that's what he wanted to say. He wanted every last bit of her, needed her, but knew that wasn't possible. To need her would ruin things, and besides, he couldn't say it. He would never say it. A woman like Aja would never go for somebody like him, not in a million years.

"Maybe veterinary school," Aja said.

She made sweeping gestures with her hands, lovely, long fingered hands. Myron was enchanted. Steering around the shore of a large, dark lake, he thought he'd never seen prettier.

"Stop," Aja said, her eyes wrinkling with mischief.

"What for?"

"I want you to stop."

Myron pulled off to the side of the road. Turn around, he expected her to say.

"Drive down there," she said, pointing to what was not more than two flattened lines in the grass.

Just back of the lake he set the parking brake and Aja sprung out her door. She darted in front of the lights, her long, dark hair snaking behind her.

"Catch me," she shouted, laughing, and lit off down the path to the lake.

Myron cut the lights and motor. He glanced around him suspiciously. He imagined four or five of the bigger dancers appearing, pulverizing the hell out of him. This had to be some kind of joke, right? But if that were the case, they were in for a very nasty surprise. Overseas, he'd discovered something frightening in himself, and these days it was just looking for an opportunity to get out.

"Aja?" he said, full of caution.

He stepped from the car, looked out over the flat, glossy water.

"Hey," he said. "Hey! Where are you?"

Aja giggled.

"Aja?"

Aja giggled again. "Don't look," she said.

And, at first, he hadn't. Then he saw her plunge into the lake. A silhouette really, but he saw her there nonetheless. Naked. Dark, smooth skin. His heart thrummed.

"Come on," she said, splashing.

Myron looked to both sides. Nettles, and he was allergic to poison ivy. He got his shirt off and looked down at his stomach. Oh well, he thought. He shucked off his shoes and pants and, bending over to hide his excitement, stepped out of his briefs.

He was feeling giddy, and the water was warm. He swam out to her. The stars were pinpricks of light overhead, the trees distant and dark on shore.

"Do you believe in magic?" Aja asked.

"I don't know," Myron said.

Aja held her hands over her head. She seemed to float there, weightless, her chin even with the water, while he dogpaddled.

"All right, I give," he demanded.

"I'm on my knees, silly," Aja laughed, standing. "There's a sandbar over here."

The water stopped just at the level of her breasts. Myron felt something open in him clear down to his feet. He had never seen anyone more beautiful.

"Come over here," she said.

He stepped up onto the sandbar. Without thinking, he kissed her. Just that. They stood looking at each other. Myron was terrified.

Aja smiled that smile.

"I was waiting for you to do that," she said.

Bzzzzzzzz, Myron's watch goes off. He pulls back the brake lever anxiously, the Monster coming around Deadman's Curve. He has been gone an eternity, it seems. The kids throw their hands up over their heads, screaming with glee. Then he has the Monster stopped, and the kids pile out. Long legs, stomping feet, grape gum. The boy at the fence watches, quiet, big-eyed.

Lost child, Myron thinks. Terrific. In a minute he'll have to call the carnival security over. But for some reason, he hesitates. Next circuit, he thinks. Then he'll call.

Myron lifts the mike, counting heads, eleven, twelve, thirteen—the boy there. Could he be? Really? He turns on the amplifier. For a moment, all he can do is stand, feeling his spiel coming on, until he grunts, launching himself into it:

It's a whirl, it's a thrill, it's a ride on the monster. No telling where it'll take you. Into the belly of the whale. Out the flaming tip of the Eternal Eye. It's anything and everything you want it to be and a whole lot more. A whole lot more, folks, whether you want it or not. Yessiree! Ride the monster. Step onto his scaly back, hang onto his mane. It's a ride you'll never forget.

Myron counts the teenagers in the holding area. Twenty, twenty-one... While he counts he rambles on. Some nights it comes out a kind of dirge, and the management tells him to cut down on the darkness and death stuff. Tonight is that kind of night.

Ride love's flaming chariot, he hears himself say, *Grip the back of the Monster and hang on. She'll toss you for all you're worth, shake your insides, rattle your brain. She'll rip out your heart and eat it, then breathe fire—*

A friend of Myron's, from his booth across the fairway, draws his hand across his throat. Cut it, Myron, he mouths, handing a kid a platter of feathered darts. Cut it!

Four tickets, Myron says, *Four tickets, folks.*

He throws the gate wide and the excited teenagers charge through. Pushing, shoving. Smell of stale beer and cigarettes and apple perfume and herbal shampoo.

"Twenty-nine," Myron says and slams the gate shut, and eyeing the boy he adds, "And one makes thirty!"

The boy shakes his head. It is a first for Myron. You little shit, he's tempted to say. Nobody passes up a freebie! He feels that old rage rise in him. He very nearly wants to weep for it.

Stop, he thinks.

"I'm gonna close my eyes and count to ten," he says. One thousand one, one thousand—"

Myron opens his eyes.

"Get the hell up there," he says, but the boy doesn't budge.

.

The night he'd done the thing he shouldn't have, they'd driven far from the fairgrounds, out into the country. By that time they'd been married a number of years.

"Come on, Aja," he said.

Sometimes, Myron knew, he could clown around a bit and shake Aja out of it—one time he'd danced in circles with light bulbs in his ears.

"I don't want to argue," he said.

Aja laughed, her teeth bright and sharp. Her laughter, this kind of laughter, made him shrivel up inside. He reached for the cigarette lighter in the dash and pushed it in for no reason. He punched the buttons in the radio and slapped the wheel. He felt alternately a terrible self-loathing, and that old rage, which had nothing to do with this thing here, now, but the rage got tangled up in it, as it did in everything:

He and the girl had wrestled in the weeds. She'd been good-looking all right, and young. There'd been a wonderful moment, all thought abandoned, bucking like a teenager, just for the joy of it, like he and Aja had that night at the lake, and then there had been—

nothing.

Nothing but this mess he'd gotten himself into. A hole in him he couldn't fathom, a lot of bad feeling in it. Maybe Lewis, he thought, over at the coin toss, would cover for him? Say he'd been repairing one of the older cars? But Lewis had gotten off early, he remembered.

"I didn't do anything," he said, trying the straightforward-lie approach. "Honest."

"Uh huh," Aja said. She dug through her purse for something to dab at her eyes. "No, not you."

What made it hard, especially hard, was that he knew she loved him, and more than he deserved. He was impossible, it seemed. Couldn't fit himself back into any kind of life.

"Honest, *really*," he said.

That did it.

"Christ!" Aja exploded. "You godamn-good-for-nothing-smart-ass-lying-son-of-a-bitch!" She was crying now. She hit him in the shoulder. The girl could really pack a punch. "You'd think you'd have the good sense not to *screw my Aunt's daughter*!" She smacked the seat with her fist. "Jesus Christ, Myron!"

This was something new. He thought he should look contrite, but couldn't conceal his shock.

"Who?"

"Gilby. Gilby, you son-of-a-bitch, is a *Coniakwe*! *Get it*?!"

Myron gripped the wheel. Something like ink darkened his brain. He felt sick. He was in for it now.You asshole! he thought to himself. And he was getting that crazy-weasel feeling, which was worse.

"I can explain," he said, but didn't.

He turned off onto a smaller road and slowed. The night was oddly reminiscent of their first. It gave things a kind of nasty irony. All week, Aja had been angry with him.

"I could rip your fuckin' head off," she said.

Myron swallowed. It was coming at him now, that crazy feeling. Bug-eyed.

"You just kept pushing me away," he said. He had to get this conversation off on another plane. Divert things. His head was cranking up like a corkscrew. He could feel it coming.

"It's been almost a month."

"Two weeks," Aja said.

"No."

"All right," she said. "Eighteen days."

Myron counted back. That helped. Counting. She was right. She'd gotten the flu a little over two weeks back. He'd held the bucket for her. It had been an altogether hot and unpleasant weekend, the Fourth.

"Hey," he said.

He made eyes and turned them on Aja. She'd told him once: You got doe eyes, that's why I love you. Your big brown eyes.

"You—" she said.

Aja slapped him. It made his eyes seem to come out of their sockets. His face stung. For a second, it was better than what he'd been feeling. He held his fists in his lap, Karate style, fingers cocked. At one time, training in Osaka, he'd broken his little fingers, each, a number of times, to get a bone build-up, to hit harder.

"Are you blind? Or just stupid?" Aja said.

"Neither," he said.

He breathed deeply, trying to calm himself. He could really hurt her if he weren't careful.

"Why are you driving so slow?" Aja asked.

Myron hadn't been paying attention; the car was barely moving. His mind was one big short-circuit. Don't hit her. Hit her. *Don't—*

"You want fast?"

Aja studied him, a harsh look in her eyes, as if he were a two-headed calf, or that Snake Woman, just another carnival monstrosity.

"You are so... *pitiful!*" she spat.

Myron put his foot to the floor. He turned to her, glaring. He wanted to tell her about those VC over there, dead VC who didn't think him pitiful at all.

"Pitiful, huh?" he spat.

The car gained speed. It was that one in the same Oldsmobile convertible they'd first gone driving in. The tie rods were bad now and the car swung from side to side. The motor roared. Telephone poles went by like slats in a picket fence. He'd kill them both.

"I'll show you pitiful!"

"Fine! Good!" Aja shouted. "Go ahead you colossal asshole! Kill us all!"

.

He'd swerved to the side of the road. The tires made a hot squealing. The car lurched to a stop. They sat like that, the motor rumbling.

"All?" Myron said.

Aja lit a cigarette. She eased back into the seat. The night was clear and quiet around them. She smiled that once beautiful, but now cruel, smile. He wanted her very badly, but was confused.

"Just wanted to see if you were listening."

A skiff of a cloud passed over the face of the moon, woolly as fleece.

"You didn't mean that, did you?" Myron asked.

"Maybe I did and maybe I didn't," she said. She stared out the windshield, making smoke rings. "What are you going to make of it?"

"You gotta tell me."

Had it been the moonlight? Or had there been an especial fullness in her face?

"I don't have to tell you anything," Aja said.

"Good," he said, his voice rising. "Then I- don't- fucking- *either!*"

"Fine!" Aja said.

Myron reached across the car and threw the door open.

"Get out!" he said.

Aja slipped across the seat.

"You're sure now," she said, hesitating, perched there in the door.

"Out," Myron said.

Aja had slid off the seat to stand beside the car.

There on the shoulder, she'd looked at him, her eyes dark and sad.

"Why, Myron?" she said. "*Why* did you do it?"

He spun the car around and roared away, watching her dwindle in the mirror.

He tore the ring from his finger—*fuck rings*, they'd called them in the army—and hurled it away. The car galloped and kicked. Bumped. When a pothole nearly threw him in a ditch, he slowed.

He bit the knuckles on his left hand, then punched the windshield, breaking it. He punched the dashboard, the door. His hand bled. He took off his T-shirt and wrapped his hand in it, the wheel slippery with blood.

"Awww, *Jesus!*" he shouted.

He was dizzy, but didn't care. What had he done? He had to have her back. He'd die without her. He was shaking. The blood stained his pants.

There was only one way.

He could do it, too: apologize.   Jesus, oh Christ, he nearly whimpered, starting the car.

Where he thought he'd let her off, he stopped.

There was a sign that shone in the moonlight: a corncob with red wings. *Dekalb*, the sign read. The rows, shoulder-high and darkly green, stretched as far as he could see. He got out of the car, stumbled down the shoulder to the ditch, his feet dragging under him.

He went up and down the length of the ditch calling—desperately.

"Aja! Annnnnn-eeeee!

Flash of candy pink neon, apple green argon, pop-tunes rising tinnily from speakers on high poles, the Monster roars and rattles, devours one gaggle of children and young lovers after another. Scores of pretty girls go by, but none of them beautiful now.

The boy watches from behind the fence, a smaller, masculine version of Aja. Myron imagines he sees Betty Davis, Aja's aunt, going by with a fluorescent pink mass of cotton candy, eyeing him at the controls. But it isn't Betty, just an older woman with big, stiff curls.

"Ride?" Myron asks the boy each circuit, trying to win him over. The boy hunkers down by the ticket booth, his eyes blinking with exhaustion.

"What's your name?" Myron finally asks, but the boy just purses his mouth and shakes his head.

Around and around the Monsters spins, light and laughter, darkness and splashing water, until somehow, no sooner than the head disappears does the tail meet it, making a scaly, green ring—lights and steam and cries of delight and fear and laughter.

Myron, wooden with fatigue, watches from the control stand, vigilant. Still, he feels it coming on, the end of this thing, begun that night.

At the trailer that night, a double-wide he'd put down on the Dibikamig lower forty, the blankets were torn, the refrigerator door left open, the light in it somehow cold, even frightening.

Aja was gone.

He flopped down on the sofa, putting his boots on the coffee table, cradling his right hand in his lap. The windows were open, the curtains billowing big and ghost-like. He studied the crusted blood across his knuckles, then snatched up the pad of paper Aja kept there. At times she wrote poems, or pieces of what she called stories, while he watched TV.

He turned the note over she'd left. Love, was pressed through the paper a number of times. He couldn't stand to read it.

He would be practical.

Repairs, he wrote, thinking of the rollercoaster he ran for the carnival. He licked the pen, as he'd seen a librarian do once.

He doodled. Then saw a graveyard, Paugook, death, dancing between headstones. He stabbed at the pad, then through it, into his leg.

Monster, he wrote across the bottom.

.

At the fair now it is late, and most of the others have gone. Fathers carry infants wrapped in blankets toward the parking area, sons and daughters in tow, mothers lugging picnic baskets and shoes and handbags. Here and there an awning flops down, red and white stripes. The popcorn wagon is boarded up. There is the rattle of plates, from the coin toss, the scrape of someone sweeping around the bumper cars.

At the Monster, the boy sleeps, his back against the backside of the ticket booth, a dragon rearing over his head, spouting flames.

Myron eyes him from the controls, where he is sending through the last bunch. Soon, most certainly, he will have to call security. They will question him.

Did he tell you his name? Did you see his parents, his mother? Why didn't you call, first thing?

No, Myron will tell them. No, no, no. And I don't know. Why don't you know? they'll ask.

Myron frowns at the thought. He realizes the absurdity of what he's been thinking. He must really be losing his mind, he thinks. He wants to hug the boy, just once—to let the boy know his father loves him.

The monster makes a rusty, mechanical shriek.

Mryon changes tracks, sends the Monster through the Tunnel of Love, then comes down from the controls to cover the boy, delicately, with his jacket. It occurs to him to remove it—what will the management think?—but instead, he squats and tucks the jacket over his shoulders, then stands back to see the boy in blue.

It is a surprise, framed this way, a shock:

He'd gotten the jacket from Aja, a souvenir of the summer she'd helped him run the resort. *Myron's Darling Resort*, the jacket reads in blue letters. Aja had suggested the name: It's funny, it's my mother's name, she said, and besides, that's the lake's name, isn't it?

Nin'imu'ce, Myron corrected her—means *sweetheart*, not Darling.

Same difference, Aja had said.

Yes, Myron thinks. Okay. *Geget*—sure.

.

Brake lever. Dynamo pedal. Buttons.

Clouds. The moon low over the lake. The rumble of the bikers headed out onto the highway, a stray bottle rocket here and there. A whoosh of sparkling light and—Pop! Tomorrow is the Fourth.

"Closed," Myron says when two scruffy-looking teenagers lean over the fence, tickets in their hands.

The crowd has thinned to nothing. On the Monster, five children scream, their parents waiting at the gate. Myron works the brake lever, slowing the monster through the Magic Mountain, and out around Deadman's curve.

Myron brings it down.

"G'night, folks," he says, as they wander off to their cars.

.

Standing with his hands on his hips, darkness all around, Myron looks for the boy. Somehow, while he was shutting down, the boy has run off, and with his jacket. He slaps his arms, chilled, but he is so numb with exhaustion, it doesn't make much difference.

He turns to look at the Monster, dark now, in part covered with green canvas, tied down with hairy ropes, shiny brass eyelets, turnbuckles and cables—and it occurs to him that everything he has built into it over the years, he has built for her.

For Aja.

And the thought comes with the power of revelation: what he was after tonight. What he'd been waiting for was to be that boy he'd been, all over again, giving his girl a rose.

But here, the rose an explanation after all these years. A testament of love.

Why, Myron, she'd asked—

See? he'd meant to say, proudly. See the way it stays on the tracks? Even though it's always just *right there*: right on the edge? Do you see how only I can run this thing? It's... *dangerous*. But See? I can control it now. I run it, see?

People have long remarked at the quality of the vampires, the gargoyles, the monsters inside. At the flame, the smoke, the noise. At the passion of the paintings, the feeling they get looking at it.

Morbid, someone once said, fantastically morbid and *wonder*fully awful. Like El Greco.

Tomorrow Clark and Sons will pack up and head for Bemidji, a few hundred miles northwest. Then on to Topeka, Kansas. Lee Summit, Missouri. Fargo, North Dakota. But this strange boy has somehow changed things. Myron is not so sure he wants to go on now.

What's the point in it, after tonight?

Still, he considers this: If he doesn't go with them, he worries, who will watch the castors on car #28? Who will touch up the paint where the cars bump into the graveyard, taking the faces off the skeletons? Who will make sure the support cables are tight enough? Who will safeguard what has taken him years to build?

Somehow, he knows, the answer is in the boy.

Lifting canvas, poking around the perimeter of the surrounding fence, looking under the wooden platform of the Monster, he feels frustrated. (Or, is it pain, an intimation of some loss he'll know later?) He would like to call out, but what? So he decides on something neutral:

"Son! *Son! You there?!*"

Calling it out, he is surprised to find his eyes glass up. From the Monster's platform, all Myron can see is shrouded in darkness. He stands, keening into the night, but hears nothing.

And like that, he hopes the boy is home. He wishes him well. He pictures warm yellow lights, windows. A small red cabin, a dock in front of it—and the thought strikes him—Aja there. The boy will give her the jacket; she'll understand, and the boy will have what he'd come for tonight.

(Why, otherwise, would a boy like that want an enormously oversized jacket stained with carnival dirt and smelling of patchouli and cigarettes?

A jacket with the word, *Nin'imu'ce*, across the back?

Loved one, sweetheart.)

Myron stands, hands on his hips, staring into the darkness, stunned.

In town, a car roars up Main, tires protesting, distant; an old tune carries in across the lake. *Mrs. Brown you've got a lovely daugh-ter!* Further south, the Burlington Northern blows its horn, a long, mournful sound, headed into the Cities.

Behind Myron the carnival, in moonlight, is skeletal. Ferris wheel, roller coaster, space needle. Myron knows he should lock the gate, and make pretenses of looking for the boy one last time—after all, he can't be entirely sure—under the booths, over by the coin toss stand, even inside the guts of the monster where, only now, without him to animate it, fright is just so much fiberglass, steel supports, hydraulic lines and wires.

He cocks his head to one side, listening. Did he hear laughter?

He lowers himself from the platform, then telling himself, he'll look for the boy, just that, he steps through the iron gate, swings it shut behind him, a final, mechanical clank, and striding out across the park, the trees rustling in the breeze, lake scent in the air, something like light blossoms in him, and with each step is a quickening, a lengthening, a pardoning rush—

Race

Summers, when I was really little, we built car traps.

On back stretches of shady, sandy road, we'd dig a pit, make a cross hatch of sticks over it, and so on, until we covered the whole mess over and went up a hillside to watch whoever was stupid enough drive down the middle and fall in. Most everybody knew to drive around to the side where the sand was funny looking. Not Officer Mullally. Heat haze shimmering off his roof, he'd roll slowly along, and just like that, drop—*thump!*—right into our hole. Three times we got him one summer. He'd try to rock his car out, tires whining, shouting "Ya Goddamn Savages!" and we'd try not to die laughing up in the pines.

Officer Mullally had *accidentally* shot a boy a few years earlier, and we were taking it out on him.

.

We were powerless and broke.

We'd been moved down from Flaming Pine, after the Big War, and the move had not been a good one. Where up north we'd worked in timber, and at resorts, as guides and cooks and mechanics, around Turtle Lake there was nothing: no farming, no industry, no rice. Tourists didn't like the reedy beaches and shallow water, and the townsfolk, miles east, didn't like us.

It was a quiet, nowhere place, and I think the BIA was hoping we'd forget to have babies and just disappear.

For a time there, nothing seemed to change except the brands of cars we drove, all twenty years old or more, and wallpaper, perhaps, and Betty Stronghold's TV.

Then, the summer I turned ten, something went crazy.

Some jackass caught a seventy pound musky offshore of our cabin, and it showed up in the St. Paul *Pioneer Press*, and by the end of May we had a huge house going up north of us, a castle almost. All summer trucks rolled in with lumber and cement, tossed up clouds of dust.

Who is that? everyone was asking.

In the fall it was saws and hammering. Winter it was quiet, but before the snow was gone, they were out again.

We went over to look. Three stories. There were marble sinks out back. Gold plated faucets. I touched one. It was cold.

Lick that, Darlene, my sister, said, and I did and my tongue stuck to that faucet.

By the end of May, they pretty much had the house all built, and then people started coming. There was a flashy sign in front.

Model Vacation Home.

A big, red-haired man with hairy knuckles bought that one. A whole bunch went up after, big hulking cabins with dormer windows and fancy roofs.

A contractor stopped by to ask us if we could kindly move the junked cars from our yard. They're an eyesore, he said. He offered to have his men move them. Won't cost you a cent, he said. My father politely told him no.

That week we went up to Big Grassy for powwow. When we got home the cars were gone.

The red-haired man, his name was Eddie Elwood. He was a doctor from down in the Cities. That June he built what looked like a small peninsula on the lake, and hauled in an enormous boat. A Chris Craft.

130

We kids all professed to hate that boat, but were thrilled when it went by. It had a car motor in it, and fins—high, and chrome-tipped. It roared like a race car, and there was Eddie at the wheel, plowing a wake across the lake four feet deep.

He was disturbing the fish, everybody said. And he was, too.

.

By that time I'd noticed something strange going on with my sister Darlene. We were all concerned over how things were changing around the lake, but Darlene was ecstatic. She'd grown out of trapping Officer Mullally's car with us, and had ceased pinning up pictures of Monty Clift and others she took a liking to at the theater in Farnsworth. Her movie magazines went under her bed.

I wondered about that. And she was smiling all the time, running off to here and there with big Nancy Koxopenace. Nancy was as round as an oil drum, but sweet, and we all liked her. Nancy and Darlene, they'd been inseparable, but now Darlene snapped at Nancy and made faces behind her back.

Darlene was sixteen that summer. I can't say she was beautiful because I'm her brother. But she turned heads. She was built in a way that was embarrassing to me. If I were in town, and if whoever was with me didn't know Darlene was my sister, they'd point, and say something, sometimes obscene. I can't recall how many times I heard, *I wouldn't kick her out of bed for eating crackers*, or, *Till the cows come home*, and all kinds of nonsense.

I was just plain sick of it.

.

And that's the way things stood when my cousin Curtis came back from his first stint in Asia, just in time for our family picnic. He'd re-enlisted, and we all wondered about that, all forty or so of us. We were sitting up on the hillside overlooking the lake. We wanted to know what he was doing over there.

"We're just advisors," he told us.

"What do you advise them?" my father asked.

"Things," he said.

"Like how the BIA gives us advice?"

"I don't think so," Curtis said.

There was a loud, whining sound. We all turned to look. Across the road, Eddie Elwood lay into a big pine tree with a chain saw. Curtis set his hands on his hips.

"What the hell's he think he's doing?" Curtis said.

He looked tough: Ray Bans, khakis, spit-shined black shoes. He was a helicopter pilot, and we were all proud of him as could be: We'd watched "Whirlybirds" on Betty Stronghold's T.V. and had all kinds of ideas of the adventures he was having overseas.

"Firewood," my father said.

A cloud of oily, blue exhaust carried across to us. Betty waved her hand in front of her face, her nose wrinkled, turned and gave Curtis a warning glance. Betty was Curtis' mother. She was the only person living, that any of us knew of, could hold Curtis back.

"I don't want you going over there," she said.

Curtis went down a little from the cabin. I followed behind him. From there we could see Eddie's dock and diving platform.

"You'd think the son-of-a-bitch owned the lake," he said.

I shrugged. "Guess so."

But, sure enough, back in those days, Eddie did, being a property owner. Laws changed that some years later, after they'd gotten more cabins running raw sewage into the lake than the lake could hold, and weeds took over and killed the fish. Then there had to be a law: Those folks from the city wanted their fish back. But that summer in 1959, there were no such laws and Eddie had staked claim there up shore.

Most of us just tolerated it: we'd had shootings and what not when the loggers went through north of us, and we'd gone to prison and they hadn't, so there didn't seem to be much point to fighting.

A breeze came up off the lake.

"Nice day," I said.

I could see Darlene and Nancy Kokopenace down on our rickety little dock, stretched out, listening to Darlene's new portable radio: it was as big as a suitcase with all kinds of dials on the front, even gold trim. I think more than a few of us wondered where she'd gotten it, but no one went so far as to say: Eddie Elwood.

But that afternoon, Darlene was on a lime green towel, Nancy on a pink. Even from up on the hillside I could feel all that with Darlene starting up in Curtis.

"What's happened to your sister there, Del?"

"Don't know," I said.

He was smiling, even with that chain saw going. He put his hand up to his forehead, like a visor.

"What's that?" he said, pointing to the boat house. You could just see the fins sticking out.

"Chris Craft," I said.

Eddie gave one last snort with his chain saw and the tree came down in a crackling rush. In the quiet you could smell the sap.

"That my motor?" Curtis said, pointing to our boat.

I nodded.

"Took me three years to pay for all that went into that motor," he said. "Look at the scow bucket it's on now."

I didn't know what to say. He was right. That Larson wasn't much of a boat. My father'd won it at a bingo game. It was painted red on the sides, making it one of the sport models, but on ours the paint was peeling and chipped, the hull concave with shovel-sized dents. The steering wheel was broken, too, the spokes sticking out, steel tipped, the windshield cracked in a way that reflected light in silvery splinters.

"Shit," Curtis said.

The year before Curtis left for Asia, he'd raced for a local bait shop. Nights you'd drive by Betty's and the light in the garage would be on, Curtis there pouring over his motor. Now it ran so poorly—backfired and popped, if it ran at all—that we seldom took our boat out.

"It goes okay," I offered.

"I'll bet it does," Curtis said, grinning.

"Well, sort of."

"Uh huh."

He was really giving Darlene a look over. That suit barely held it all in.

"Ah, screw it," he said. "Wouldn't've been any good just collecting dust anyway. Bet you're right."

Eddie came down the hillside opposite us and stood on his dock. He had that white skin red-haired people have, and he stood with his shoulders pulled back, his stomach sucked in. He was looking at Darlene, too. He said something and Nancy laughed. Darlene sat up, propped on her elbows. She spun around, kicking her feet in the water. Eddie splashed back at her. It was pretty clear just then, what was between them.

"Well, isn't he a prince," Curtis said.

"You watch it there," Betty said. She'd snuck up behind us. Bart Kills-In-Sight was with her. He smiled uncomfortably.

"Come on and fill up, Mr. War Hero," Bart said.

He took Curtis by the arm and led him to the table and everybody eating there. Betty slapped a portion of beans and venison on Curtis' plate.

"Now *siddown*!" Betty said.

There was the Clang! Clang! of horseshoes behind the cabin. Misha, a Russian who'd built a shack down by the Finedays, came up with his rifle and we gave him some venison. Between mouthfuls he rambled on about Siberia, where he said we would all be going if we didn't listen to him.

"We *are* in Siberia," Curtis said testily.

Mischa grunted.

"He's touched," I told Curtis.

"Really?" Curtis said.

Everybody settled in on the hillside there, eating. My father came back from horseshoes. Some of the older relatives were swapping stories.

"This is boring as hell," Curtis said, and stood.

I followed him down to the lake. It made me a little anxious, how he balled his hands into fists. We turned the corner around the last of the

134

sandy banks and there was the dock, but no Nancy or Darlene. We went up to the end there, looked around.

There was a throaty rumble. Curtis turned.

"That's it," I said.

Eddie eased his Chris Craft out from his boat house. It was longer than a car, all shiny and white and chrome, exhaust curling behind it.

"Jesus," Curtis said.

"I know," I said.

We both turned to look at our old Larson. Curtis kicked it. It gave a dull, aluminum thud.

"Hey! *Chingus!*" Betty called down. Weasel. "Don't you do anything now."

Everybody was up there. The Finedays and Jacksons and Strongholds and a few stragglers. I remember the way Curtis smiled:

Whirlybirds, I thought.

Eddie Elwood roared by, turning so his wake splashed up over our shoes. Darlene's hair streamed out behind her, thick as a horse's tail and shiny black. The boat pounded over some waves, thump, thump-thump-thump! That was one tiny swimsuit, and Darlene was moving in it.

Eddie smiled that smile Curtis had, something ugly in it.

The third time around, Eddie slowed. Carroty red hair. Thick fingers on the wheel. A yellow shirt with green parrots on it. The exhaust burbled. Darlene smiled, too, now. Squarish, white teeth.

Nancy waved. "Hey, Curtis!"

"Race you in that skunk boat," Eddie shouted. He slid by the dock, heavy in the water.

"That boat of yours is just an old sow," Curtis said.

"Come on then," Eddie said. "Let's have a little race. Me and the north end against you and the south."

My heart give a jerk. All those cabins had gone up north of us.

"Wouldn't want to waste my time," Curtis said.

"Okay," Eddie shot back. He smiled real free and easy, and just like that, wrapped his arm around Darlene's bare shoulders. Dead-fish-white on brick skin.

I got a sick, twisted feeling in my stomach. I'd wondered how she'd come up with the money for that radio, too. But now it was all right in front of me. Curtis' mouth puckered.

"You're on, Asshole," he shouted.

He dropped down into that old Bingo-bought Larson. He started throwing everything out. I couldn't catch it all. Life preservers, extra gas, Folgers cans full of dirt and worms, cane poles; some of it went right over my head and into the water. Plosh! Plosh! Plosh-plosh!

Curtis was talking to himself. "Fucking goddamn son-of-a-bitch."

He threw out one thing after another until there was nothing in that boat but him. He even took the cowling off the motor and untied the anchor and dropped it over the side.

"You can find it later," he said.

I wasn't about to argue with him.

By that time, Eddie had gotten to the far end of the lake and was waiting. It was a small lake, not much more than a mile long and narrow. Curtis rolled back his sleeves and took off his shoes. Betty and the others came down.

"What's all the fuss?" she said.

I knew to keep my mouth shut.

"Curtis," she said.

"George," Curtis said to my father. "Mind if I use your boat?"

"Your motor's on it," my father said. "You can do what you want."

"What are you all waiting for?" Curtis said.

We all stood back.

Curtis got down on his knees, turned some screws in there with his jackknife. He pulled on the starter rope and that motor coughed into life, then roared—Betty put her hands over her ears it was so loud. Curtis grabbed one of the dock poles and pushed himself away from shore. The motor popped twice, then caught and the sound just about raised the hairs on your neck—it was a kind of scream.

That boat flashed silver and red, Curtis angling around to the north end where Eddie was waiting. The two of them bobbed there, exchanging insults.

The water shimmered.

When they finally turned south, there was an awful tearing and roaring and they came up the lake, Eddie's Chris Craft throwing tall gouts of water, our Larson bouncing along beside it.

They were head to head passing us, but just a block or so off the far shore, Curtis let that thing go, and like squirting a watermelon seed from between your fingers, that boat got right up on the propeller and flew.

Beat Eddie by a boat length.

It was tricky going, almost impossible; we could all see that. Curtis was a pilot, all right. That's what we all said.

My father went to the end of the dock and flagged him down. But they were at it again. At the north end, Curtis pulled the same trick, but too late, and Eddie shook his fist over his head, victorious.

So they had one length to go: best out of three. And now there were waves and it was trickier. But infinitely more so for Curtis. Even Bart, who'd driven his station wagon for years without brakes, looked sick.

"Wish he'd call it quits," he said.

We heard that roar and whine—you could even feel it in the sand. Waves pummeled the shore. None of us cheered or carried on.

Betty crossed herself. Bart cursed.

Like the time before, Eddie was in front, his big hands around the wheel. Darlene sat stock still next to him, her eyes wide. We couldn't see Nancy. She must have been crouching behind the seat.

Going by, it was close.

We could all see Curtis was about to stand that boat on her tail. He's crazy, I thought, and felt a swelling of pride. Jesus! I thought.

And just as I did, as we all did, he squirted out again, passed him fair and clear, and Eddie, seeing how he'd lost, swerved and hit Curtis broadside with his wake. Curtis skipped across the water like a stone— end over end over end—to crash down one last time, hull upside down and no Curtis swimming out from under.

I felt my mouth hanging open.

"Curtis!" Betty shouted.

Bart ran up the road, my father behind him. Eddie looped around shore. He was trying not to grin.

Betty shook her fist. "Get out there!"

Eddie was just taking his good old time turning around. Darlene was crying. Nancy threw herself over the side and flopped in toward our dock.

"So help me I'll rip your goddamned head off!" Betty shouted at Eddie.

But it was no use. None of it was, and when Officer Mullally made it out the following morning, he blamed the whole thing on Curtis.

For a long time after the lake was quiet.

But the movement of the vacationers up from the Twin Cities had started, and was irreversible, and Turtle Lake was never the same.

I'd gotten just a taste of it: the cool, echoing silence. Wood smoke rising slowly on grey rainy evenings. A loon calling from across the lake.

It was so quiet you could hear the Burlington Northern going through Farnsworth, down to the Cities.

It made a sad, far off whistling.

Had Eddie got out to Curtis right away, some of my relatives argued, he would have made it. But the truth was, one of the spokes in that steering wheel pierced Curtis' left ventricle and that was that.

The coroner told us.

My father and Bart pulled him out from under our boat, even worked him over on shore, breathed air into him, but he was dead.

I remember standing over Bart and my father. My bare feet in the hot sand. Their grunts and cries. It all seemed miles away.

Betty wept.

We all stood over Bart and my father, Curtis there staring up into eternity.

Now there are paved roads into Little Turtle, and you'd never know it had been a reserve. Everybody sold out, and they cut down those big trees and it's bright and cheery. There's even a bait shop and marina on the north end. Big pumps like at a gas station and fluorescent lights and dirty magazines in the racks behind the counter and fifteen kinds of ice cream.

We laid Curtis down at the nearby game reserve. We knew nobody would bother him there. Even made a grave house for him and decorated it with hawk feathers. I was there.

"That boy could really fly," Bart said.

The following fall, I was there, too, when Eddie Elwood, trimming the pines that blocked his view of the lake, fell on his chain saw and cut himself.

Nothing would stop the bleeding, and Betty went to the bait store on the North End and called for Officer Mullally, while Eddie's wife stayed at his side. Coming down Maple, Mullally went into a washout he said, later, was deeper than a goddamn grave. He got stuck there, and had to carry his first aid kit in on foot. By the time he got to Eddie's cabin, though, Eddie had bled to death.

We were all real sorry, and said as much to his wife.

Officer Mullally, bent over Eddie's body with that tourniquet, gave me and Darlene and Nancy a deep down dirty look. From our side of the road, we grinned in return, sick at ourselves. By then Darlene was well into her sixth month and showing pretty bad.

"Put him in the back of my car," Mullally said, and moments later pulled out.

We never built another sand trap. I guess that's the way it goes.

And the boat? My father took the steering wheel off. The rest of them thought it pretty gruesome, but whenever I got the chance, I went down and sat in the back, making exhaust noises.

Mr. Motorman, they called me.

It didn't matter that I found out Curtis'd never gotten near a helicopter, or that he hadn't been a pilot.

I saw Curtis there, hand on the throttle.

And for just a little, tiny time, I was carried along with him, free and above it all, flying in the face of what was for all of us, the end.

4

What It All Comes To

Rhubarb

Their first mistake, Dalton told his wife Carol that evening over dinner, pointing his fork in mock accusation, had been to leave Carol's mother, Teddy, to watch over the house the week they'd been gone. That, right there, Carol's wonderful idea, he said—that had started it all.

"I mean, look at this—" he said.

Dalton ducked his head around the light fixture, which hung between them. It had hung there for years, spring loaded so you could raise or lower it, but higher, up near the ceiling. Now, Teddy had broken it, too, along with a dozen things around the house.

How did she do it? Teddy was that odd sort of woman who, when the functioning of something weren't obvious, took it to task.

It would have made them laugh, but she'd cannibalized the answering machine, too, which was crucial to their business. Dalton was an architect, Carol did drafting, both from the office in their home.

When Dalton had asked Teddy, in as measured a voice as possible, why the ingoing and outgoing tapes had been reversed, Teddy had told them it was all too complicated, and she'd written down the calls anyway.

Had she been gone from the house? Dalton asked. Teddy had not answered. She'd been telling them, almost ecstatically, about her week, the university fund-raiser dinners and her part in them as keynote speaker. She was professor emerita in Classics, after all, she'd tell people. She'd use that as an excuse for breaking things—her not belonging to the modern and, as she put it, *inelegantly complicated*, world.

But it wasn't any of the things she'd broken in the house that was at issue between Carol and Dalton now, it was how Dalton's and Teddy's interactions had become hostile.

"You shouldn't have talked to her like that, all icy and nasty," Carol said, "after all, she was doing us a favor."

"No," Dalton said, "we were doing her a favor. Remember? She just happened to arrange to have her kitchen and bathroom painted while we were gone?"

"So what was our second big mistake?" Carol asked.

Dalton hadn't thought of a second thing, hadn't been making an argument of it, but he did now.

"Telling her to water the plants," he said, and then corrected himself. "No," he said, "telling her to water the plants and watch for bugs on the rhubarb."

Just then both Dalton and Carol laughed, their eyes glassing up. It wasn't just that Teddy's attentions had killed the rhubarb, but the way she'd done it that amused them. Dalton faked a punch at the hanging light.

"Always wanted a punching bag for a light. It's trendy, take those inches off my waistline. And—" he grinned behind it, "—when your mother comes over, you two can sit over there and I can take time out behind the bag, what do you say?"

And here, Dalton threw a combination at the light, and striking it, the light swung out, then back, clanking into his glasses. The light rocking, Dalton feigned a change-up, mimicked Howard Kosell's voice:

"He's on the ropes, and what a fight it is! He's try-ing to make it back up but—oh, folks! He's taken another left to the eye!"

For a moment both of them sobered, thinking this thing through. Dalton had, when he'd seen the rhubarb—so withered as to be nearly unrecognizable—said things to Teddy he'd have been better off not saying. He told himself now, it was the time and effort he'd put into the rhubarb that had made him explode, get mean—if that's what they were going to call it.

He'd gone to great lengths to have the variety shipped in, all the way from Ontario, Canada Red, instead of Victoria Green or Crimson Cherry, and he'd cut back the lilacs, brought in sand, a half ton of it, mounded the sand the way the greenhouseman had instructed. The greenhouseman had also told him to keep the bugs away with something called Liquid Seven. Dalton had kept it locked in a cupboard over his garage workbench.

And babied by Dalton, the rhubarb had flourished, until Teddy had seen "Oh, some bugs or another," and had gone on the attack. Only, she hadn't used the Liquid Seven. All this, Dalton had explained to Carol as explanation for his bad behavior. The digging, and the awful carting of sand, his aching back. And finally, what Teddy had done.

"I'm glad we don't have a cat," Dalton said.

At the table, they laughed again. Fits of laughter. It was ridiculous, all of it!

Teddy. The house. The rhubarb.

"Let's get her a job in interior design," Dalton said, "my clients would love her! She could antique a house in hours!"

"Stop it," Carol said and Dalton led her upstairs, both of them laughing like they hadn't since they'd been students, punch drunk with lack of sleep in design class, and he'd won her over.

.

But it wasn't so funny the following day, nor the day after, when Teddy still would not return their calls.

Now, in the middle of dinner, Carol, tried to reach her again.

Dalton watched her in the kitchen from behind the light. While Carol was waiting with the phone pressed to her head, he stood and knotted the light cord double. Carol's brows furrowed, and she glanced at Dalton, setting the phone down.

At the table, she picked at her chicken salad.

"What exactly *did* you say to her out there?"

The afternoon they'd returned, Carol had been at the picture window, and had only seen Dalton and her mother arguing, but she'd recognized that behavior in Dalton she most disliked immediately, his *forensics* posture. Dalton had a sharp wit, which he used in a self-deprecating, and amusing way, one Carol usually enjoyed, but occasionally, if he were really pushed, he could use it to... *eviscerate* people, she'd said to him once. Now she was hoping he hadn't done that with her mother.

"Did you say something about... *popsicles* to Teddy?" Carol asked.

Dalton caught himself blinking.

"You did say something, didn't you," Carol said.

Dalton fixed what he thought was a pleasant look on his face.

"What?"

Once a week, Teddy had them over for dinner, usually Friday, and the food was—well, Dalton thought, the food wasn't the point of it, but still—

"I want to hear it," Carol said.

Dalton looked up from his plate. "I told her if she had to make popsicles she'd burn them."

Carol stared. "What did Teddy say?"

"She told me you didn't bake popsicles."

"And what did you say?"

Dalton didn't answer.

"What did you say, Dalton?"

"I asked her if she'd read that on the package, or if she'd discovered it herself."

Carol threw down her napkin and went to the phone. She tried again, but still her mother wouldn't answer.

"You're going to fix things with Teddy, when I get her on the line," Carol said.

Dalton only nodded, and bent to his dinner like a condemned man at his last meal.

.

A short while later, they were in the car outside Teddy's one story ranch in an outlying suburb. Dalton could see Teddy moving inside through her yellow chintz curtains. The house was a shade of peach that made him think of flesh, like on a plastic doll. It was an awful color, and he thought, you'd nearly have to be blind to choose something like it. Still—

"After all these years, why did you do it, Dalton?" Carol said.

They were waiting for Dalton to get out of the car. Once out of the car, he would walk to the front door, and there ring, and when Teddy answered, apologize and ask her to come over for dinner the following evening. Since she'd disconnected her phone, he was here on her step, he'd explain.

They were having pineapple upsidedown cake, he was to tell her. Her favorite.

In the car, Dalton's tongue almost stuck to the back of his throat thinking about it: Teddy liked everything so sweet it was almost inedible. One time she'd told him to put pineapple in his orange juice, and if he wanted it to be especially good, give it a *dollop of sugar, a tablespoon or so,* just to cut the sour orange flavor.

Dalton sat at the wheel, drumming his fingers on the dashboard.

"I can't do it," Carol said. "I'm not the one who attacked her." She tossed her hair back over her shoulders. "And I still can't understand why you did."

Dalton stopped his drumming. A cool, early June breeze blew the scent of lilacs through the car. He wondered himself. Why not just go in now and apologize?

Dalton, thinking, frowned. It was complicated, for what Carol did not know was this: for years, Teddy and Dalton had traded barbs, all in good fun. To Dalton's, "What color is your hair this week?" Teddy would respond, "I'll just have to check my reflection in your bald spot and see. It's gotten shinier, do you use some kind of polish?" They might keep this sort of thing up for minutes, then give each other a peck on the cheek. "Nice to see you, Lady Macbeth," Dalton would say, and Teddy would reply, "The pleasure is all mine, Iago."

Carol had never been party to these exchanges, they would have upset her.

But Dalton sensed something had gone amiss now in their last exchange of acerbic repartee. His barb that afternoon, about the popsicles, had gone unreturned and, somehow, instead of continuing their old banter, he'd wounded Teddy, and he doubted this creeping around her door and apologizing was the way to right things.

Teddy, he knew, beneath that veneer of sharp humor, was a sensitive and private person. Now Dalton suspected she needed to tell them something, but couldn't.

"So, you won't do it," Carol said, shaking her head.

"I didn't say that," Dalton said.

"But you won't. I know you."

"Let's not be too hasty on this one," he replied.

"You were pretty hasty when you said what you did."

"Did you see that rhubarb? Not to mention the rest of the garden? Those were elephant ears there in that dirt, not rhubarb leaves, sweetie."

Both of them had to laugh. The garden, when they'd returned, had been wilted nearly beyond saving, but the rhubarb, off by itself, had long since passed, the enormous leaves gray-brown and paper dry.

"This is stupid," Dalton said. "Look, she's got us out here in the car, she can see us through those curtains of hers. I'm sure she knows we're out here. We care, we'll get to it when our tempers cool, right?"

Carol considered this, her eyes narrowing.

"And what am I really saying I'm sorry for?" Dalton said. "I mean, *she's* the one who poured Liquid Plumber on my rhubarb."

"She didn't mean to."

"Well, she poured it on your goddamn dieffenbachia too, or didn't you notice?"

"She thought it was plant food, or insecticide or whatever," Carol said, and shifting in her seat added, "Or, that's what she said, anyway."

Dalton set his hands on either side of the wheel, his arms outstretched. He was thinking, both containers had been the same color, but still, no one, but no one, with two good eyes in her head, could mistake Liquid Plumber, with that skull and crossbones on the label, for Liquid Seven, with its sunflower logo.

But Teddy had.

Something awful sunk in Dalton's stomach. The reasons she might make such a mistake weren't pleasant to consider. Carol gave him a stern look.

"Are you going or not?"

Just then, Teddy threw the chintz curtains open. She was a well-kept woman, always in blue, and she was in blue now, her hair done up elaborately.

Dalton waved to her, but she just glared out into the street, frowning.

"See?" Dalton said. "I told you she was too mad to accept an apology," and with a grimace, as much at himself for having gotten into this stupid mess, as for anything, pulled away from the curb.

That Friday, after dinner, Dalton managed to get Teddy on the phone.

Carol was reading on the sofa. Carol hadn't asked him to call, he'd just had it. He didn't want the weekend to spin out into some ridiculous unpleasantness. And his mind was making the worst now out of what could have gone wrong with Teddy. A stroke? Early dementia?

"Hi, Teddy," he said when she answered. "It's Jerry."

"Who?" she said.

For a moment he was dumbstruck. Did she really not know who he was?

"Dalton," Dalton said. "Jerry Dalton.' He stopped himself from saying, Your son-in-law, the guy that married your daughter?

"I thought we could stop this nonsense," he said, and then, gritting his teeth, added, "I mean, Thanks for taking care of the house while we were gone."

There was a hum on the line.

"Oh, sure," Teddy said, brightly. "If you need me again just let me know. I'll feed the canaries, too."

Dalton didn't know what to say to that; he felt as if he'd been kicked. Of course, they didn't have canaries. But then, he hadn't said he was sorry, either.

"Well," he said. "By all means don't forget the dog; his digestion's been a little slow and your addition to his diet would help immeasurably. Get things moving, if you know what I mean."

Dalton, gripping the phone, cringed at himself. In his intimating how she'd used the Liquid Plumber on his rhubarb was a meanness, a smallness that shocked him.

"Well, since you're not big enough to say what's to be said in situations such as this one, I'm going to hang up now," Teddy said, and she did just that.

Minutes later, Teddy called, and though Dalton answered it, all she said to him was,

"My daughter there?"

Dalton got a book, a thriller he'd been reading, and sat on the sofa. Carol and Teddy talked for some time, and even though the book was the kind you could read on a beach, or at an amusement park for that matter, Dalton couldn't follow a word.

Then Carol was back. She patted his arm and kissed him.

"I'm glad you two are all patched up," she said, and Dalton, not wanting to disappoint her, or was it, ruin their weekend, grinned.

He felt just then a kind of dread. It persisted through the night and, even after a beer or two, had him tossing uneasily in bed until he slept.

In the middle of the night, Dalton woke. He reached for his glasses and couldn't find them. Carol lay with her back to him under the covers.

He was staring into the dark, having wakened from a dream that had his heart pounding. In it, he'd held a book close to his face, but no matter how hard he squinted, he couldn't read the print. An exam was to be given on the book and there he sat, under cockeyed and broken lamps, unable to so much as make out a word of it.

In the dark, he began to sweat. Something began to come clear to him, and what it was made his stomach knot. All these years he'd been amused at Teddy's breaking things, the rods on the Venetian blinds, the stereo, a toaster, the rotisserie, and now the dining room fixture and answering machine.

Teddy hated machines, and they seemed to respond in kind, waging war with her. But in all these years, never, never had she nearly killed herself with a mixture of lye and bleach; never had she really used the wrong spices in her dinners—they had always just been so beastly salty and over-cooked, to his and Carol's taste. But the rhubarb, she hadn't been able to hide that.

Still, how in the world had she mistaken Liquid Plumber for the insecticide? In a snit, after he'd made the popsicle comment, she'd gone inside, had complained about the "new" glasses she was wearing, and how difficult it was to adjust to them.

And in the dark, Dalton realized the problem was not in his mother-in-law's glasses. Or her mind.

Now, Dalton saw if he was right, it was incredible what Teddy had managed. And she'd done it in a way that hadn't aroused suspicion. That she'd given up her car in the last year to take the bus if she went anywhere other than the grocery store he'd figured for her dislike of the heavier traffic in the Twin Cities. And though she'd never watched TV, but now always had hers on, he'd attributed to her having gotten cable and premium channels that were of interest to her. Teddy had said as much.

Yet, just this spring, he'd pointed a bird out to Teddy, a sparrow, when he and Carol had stopped in front of her house in the car to drop her off.

"Is that the Horn-beaked triple-crowned warble weaver you've been telling us has been at your feeder?" he'd asked, joking.

That Teddy had not responded in kind, he realized now, had been the first deviation from their usual banter. So, even back then.

"You point over here, over there," Teddy had replied, with great indignation. "How am I supposed to see up your arm and your finger when you're weaving all over the place like some common drunk," she'd said, and had charged into the house.

He'd had a glass more wine at dinner than he supposed he should, but still, the remark had stung.

Now Dalton reached under the bed for his glasses, brushed his fingers one direction and then the other over the plush carpet. He looked on the night stand, the dresser, but without them on he couldn't see to find them, just now one of those odd ironies. And he wouldn't wake Carol by turning on the light.

Not now.

He pulled on his pants, shirt, and shoes, and crossing the room, stepped on his glasses—he must have knocked them off the night stand—bending the frames. He jammed them on his face, adjusting them as best he could, just now satisfied with them crooked in a way he never would have been earlier.

He let himself out the front door, then paused on the stoop. It was just getting light out, and he saw the wash of light in the clouds on the horizon for the miraculous thing it was, layer upon layer of pink, and orange, and yellow cloud.

Across the street from him, the houses he usually disliked, painted in pastels, blue and coral and teal, seemed nothing short of a wonder, vivid, their sharp rooflines and dormers pleasing.

Dalton got in his car, then drove to a convenience store and bought the sweet rolls in the counter that had the most icing on them, and in the dairy case, lifted out a whole half-gallon of pineapple juice.

In Teddy's driveway, he stopped the car and sat a moment. He knew Teddy would be up, even after quitting her job with the university, which she'd done far earlier than she'd said she would—taking early retirement, and a smaller pension—which had been a mystery to Carol and Dalton, but he understood that now, too.

All that thorny behavior of the last year, made sense now.

He waited in the car a minute, then, taking the bag, went to the door and rang the bell. Teddy put her face in the tiny window set in the middle of the door.

"Who is it?" she demanded. She was looking right into Dalton's face.

"Who is it?" she said again, and after enough time to make his point clear, Dalton told her.

.

Inside, Dalton set the table and poured the pineapple juice. Teddy sat across from Dalton; she ate slowly. They talked about the weather, and how the local baseball team was doing, how the roses were out now, all as if they commonly had breakfast together at this time in the morning, barely after dawn. Then Dalton lapsed into silence, and Teddy followed.

After a time she looked up at Dalton.

"I'm sorry about the... *rhubarb*," she said, grinning bravely, this her offering of peace, a joke. "Carol doesn't do well with bad news, you know. She was always like that, crying and carrying on, even when she was...."

"I know," Dalton said.

Dalton went around the table and sat in the chair beside Teddy. He wanted to know how bad it was. Teddy obliged. She moved her face closer to Dalton's until she was just inches away, then nodded, touching his glasses with her hands, something final in it, and abruptly sat back.

And just then, she did something Dalton would always, later, remember.

"Your glasses are all... bent out of shape," Teddy said, her voice quavering just the slightest. "Is that a new style, a fashion statement or something, or are you trying to tell me something?"

She grinned at him, this silence in the room. Dalton reached for her, and she put her hand over his. Her eyes had glassed up, big rheumy, nearly blind eyes. Dalton's heart kicked in his chest.

He knew he had to say something, something amusing, but what? What could he say?

"Junkyard Modern," Dalton said, as it came to him, a burning in his throat. "I'll get you a pair, I promise. They won't take you long to break in," Dalton said. "You can break them in in your own sweet time.

"All right, Teddy? Is that all right?"

Teddy pressed his hand. "And you'll tell Carol?" she asked.

"I'll see to everything," Dalton said, and Teddy, with a sigh, smiled.

The Sixth Monkey

Step down off that star, darlin', and daddy'll give you *anything* you want," Burke said.

Mayellen, Burke's daughter, was winding up to cry again. All of five, in a pink dress and black patent leather shoes, she was stuck in the center of the Universe Game at the Clark County Fair and wouldn't be budged from the Big Dipper. Burke smiled so broadly he felt his face might split.

"What's wrong, honey?" he asked, though he was all too well aware of the reason. His visitation was nearly over, his first in a number of months, and the next would be equally far off, to Mayellen an eternity.

"We gotta go—" Burke said, but this only served to make Mayellen glare all the harder. Across the immense board, all sparkling silver light and orange comets, others turned to watch.

"Mayellen," Burke nearly whispered, "come on now."

Mayellen's face reddened, and a wail, piercing and long, escaped from her, shrill as a steam whistle.

Burke leapt over the partition. He swung Mayellen off the lighted platform, and cradling her, as he once had an infinite number of footballs, something like a siren and a flashing red light going off behind him, he charged out of the Universe Game and into the crowd, decisive, himself again.

And here Mayellen was smiling, moments later, pink cloud of sticky cotton candy on a blue cone, her face smudged with artificial color. Burke glanced at his watch. They were fifteen minutes late, and Sandra, his estranged wife, if anything, was punctual. They would have to turn back, should have already. Still, walking now, Mayellen's small, sweaty hand in his, each moment bled into the next, and he could not, just plain *could not* let go. Burke anxiously looked up the crowded midway. "Ah, hell," he said. Somewhere out there, in the jostle of people and bright lights, Sandra was searching for them, hands clenched into fists, he imagined, her face twisted in that way he so disliked.

"Daddy?" Mayellen said.

Burke, for just a moment, felt his eyes glass up, his throat swell painfully, at the sound of it. *Daddy*. Burke, a trader in volatile market commodities, in all his years, had never felt so helpless as he did now.

"What, honey?" he said.

They turned up a long, narrow aisle of tents, the night coming on. Overhead, the sky had gone royal blue, and the stars came out pinpricks of light.

"Does anything hold the stars up?" Mayellen asked.

Again, Burke's eyes burned. He squeezed his daughter's small, sticky hand in his own. Burke had to think. He had not seen Mayellen in nearly four months. Should he say, gravity? Or should he say, angels, angels hold them up? What had Sandra been telling her, aside from the usual (that he got overly excited at times, was given to impulses, and that he would not keep promises he made)?

"What do you think?" he asked.

"I think they're just stuck up there," Mayellen said, but saying it she gripped his hand.

"Is that what your momma says?"

The girl frowned. Burke's heart thrummed. *There*, he'd gone and done it. He'd violated the rules of their little game, had used that word: momma. But Mayellen skipped ahead, tugging at Burke.

"I want a monkey," she said.

Here, in front of them, was a baseball toss, a greasy-haired carnie head to toe tattoos, calling, "Dollar a ball, can't miss, everybody's a winner!"

A row of smiling monkeys leered at waist level, prizes, the smallest on the left, no bigger than Burke's thumb, the biggest, on the right, nearly life-sized, hairy with bright purple fur. Burke tugged at his daughter's hand. He had given himself an ultimatum: thirty minutes, yet here they had used them.

"You promised," Mayellen said.

"I know I did, honey," Burke replied. "But I got you that cotton candy."

"But it's gone," Mayellen said.

Burke cringed. That he had neglected to send Mayellen birthday or Christmas gifts—he'd been on the road, on business—came powerfully to him now.

"I could *keep* a monkey, "Mayellen said.

Burke eyed the carnie and the bottles on the raised platform at the back of the booth. The game was a dupe, Burke knew that. The pyramids of what looked like milk bottles were really wooden facsimiles weighted with lead, or some heavy metal. Or there was some trick in the way the bottles were elevated.

"Give 'er a go," the carnie said. 'Can't lose, everybody's a winner. Give 'er a go. One toss can't hurt, and the little lady wants a monkey."

Burke slapped a crumpled five on the counter and the carnie pushed a number of balls across. Burke palmed the first, worked the stitching with his nails. He stepped back from the booth, warming up his arm, then hurled the ball, knocking over the pyramid of bottles.

"You win!" the carnie hooted, and handed Burke the smallest monkey on the left.

Burke, ecstatic, was about to give Mayellen the monkey, when she stamped her foot.

"But I want *that* one," she said, pointing to the biggest on the right.

"Get out of the way, you," Burke said, pushing the carnie to his left.

.

He'd knocked down enough of the bottles to work himself up to the fourth monkey, the medium-sized, green-haired monkey, and was settling himself to go after the fifth. In the stall, lights blinked off and on, red, green, and yellow. Bells rang. There was a confusing point system to the thing, but Burke ignored it. Behind, and to his left, Mayellen watched, carefully nibbling at what was left of her cotton candy.

"Daddy?" she said.

"Just a second, hon," Burke shot back.

.

He was in it, he was riding it, he had this thing nailed, he was sure of it. It would take just a little more adjustment, more top spin, or would a curve do it? Burke wound up, as he had all those years playing league ball, and knocked over all but one bottle of yet another set.

"Another five?" the carnie jabbed.

Burke slapped down the money. He'd spent forty dollars, all the cash he had, and had written a check for more. He corralled the balls possessively against the biggest monkey on the right.

Maybe he'd stand further back?

.

Mayellen tugged at Burke's leg.

"I like the green one, Daddy," she said. "I like green better than orange."

"No you don't," Burke said, making a sweep of the row of monkeys. "You want the big one, the purple one on the end there. That's what you said, sweetie."

"But—"

The Carnie not so subtly spit in Mayellen's direction, and she sidled off to the left, perplexed by his whistling a tune she knew from school, "Yankee Doodle Dandy."

"Daddy?" Mayellen asked, but Burke was settling into another pitch.

.

Somewhere into winning the fifth monkey, the orange monkey, standing back from the booth, naked to the waist and sweating, a crowd

158

there, firing balls off as if he were on a mound, pitching, Burke heard a woman's voice: "Excuse me. *Excuse me? Let me through?*"

Burke, dizzy with exertion, stopped to focus on the woman. Stiff blond hair, blue eye-shadow. She cocked her head to one side, pointing. Burke looked. Mayellen lay against the booth, fast asleep, her arms wrapped tightly around herself. Burke, as if waking, took himself in: bare gut and white upper arms, sweaty shirt tied around his middle. Behind him, the carnival goers—dirty jeans, torn T-shirts, and bright caps—waited.

"You aren't quittin', are ya?" the carnie asked. "The next'll be your lucky ball there. Jackpot. Sevens, all across."

Burke stooped to sweep Mayellen up.

He was thinking of some choice things to say—about jackals, or carrion, or vultures—but said none of them. Instead, Mayellen cradled in his arms, he turned on his heel and headed up the midway.

"Hey! Hey, Buddy! You forgot your monkey!" the carnie called after him, laughing.

At the Space Bullet, a machine that whisked two pointed-nosed cabs around a lighted axle, Burke sat with Mayellen. The air was heavy with the smell of popcorn and electricity and grease and the cheap perfumes and colognes of the carnival goers. Burke's hair was slick with sweat, but combed back, and his shirt on and straightened, though his tie was askew. Mayellen fidgeted with her shoelaces, the orange-haired monkey between them. Neither Burke nor Mayellen touched it. They had been waiting nearly twenty minutes, but then, they were a good two hours late. Sandra, no doubt, would be furious, was furious.

Burke ran his fingers through his hair, trying to make himself more presentable. What he'd done struck him as very nearly crazy now and he was afraid he looked it. Burke had always thought he could control what his wife called his "compulsions"—only, as he'd seen it, there'd never been occasion to do so. It had always been just more business, a better life, more free time *later.* But now, waiting, he had cause to consider the things she'd been saying. He was *confused*, she'd said. You fix yourself on something and then go after it long after the cost is too great. You lack a sense of proportion, she'd said. This is life, not college football. Don't you see the difference?

Burke, earlier, had just written that kind of thinking off to the difference between men and women, the way they thought of things. But tonight— Two hours late! His face in his hands, he could barely look at Mayellen, though, surely, she'd seen him as oblivious of her before. He peeked at her between his fingers, abashed, trying to make light of it all.

"It's okay, daddy," she said.

Burke dropped his hands. "What's okay, sweetie?"

"That you didn't win the sixth monkey."

The girl's legs didn't quite reach the ground and she swung them back and forth playfully. Burke looked out over the parking lot, lights veering there in bright arcs, every moment expecting the police, or Sandra, in a rage, coming up the midway, through all these people.

"I really like orange better," Mayellen said.

Burke set the monkey in his lap and pulled Mayellen to his side, wrapping his arm around her. Compulsive, Sandra had said. But he knew what she'd meant: *Sick.*

Burke propped his chin on the monkey's head, waiting.

In a fluster, and striding purposefully, but on shaky legs—even at a distance Burke could see that—Sandra came up the midway, a little after ten, through the young toughs in their rockwashed jeans and fluorescent T-shirts, through the parents and kids.

"I was worried sick," Sandra said.

She'd cut her hair short, one of those asymmetrical things, and Burke caught himself studying her. It looked good, except it made her ears stick out. She put her hand on Burke's shoulder, and gave him a peck— it surprised Burke, she'd been hostile for so long—then scooped Mayellen into her arms and squeezed her.

"I'm sorry—I am *so* sorry," Sandra said.

Burke could see she was doing her best not to collapse against him. He could tell these things about her. She smelled nice. How had he not noticed, this last year, just how pretty she was—beautiful, really.

"What happened?" Burke asked.

He did not mean it as a lie, did not mean to imply they'd been waiting all this time for her. He was truly concerned. Sandra pointed to the car parked across the highway. The rear of it was caved in.

"Some idiot hit me," she said. "I was pulling out of Byerly's, that grocery? And he just hit me." Mayellen shifted and Sandra smiled at her.

"Are you okay?" Burke asked.

Already his head was in high gear. He would call his lawyer, call their doctor. "Tell me everything," Burke said.

"I'm *fine*," Sandra said. She kissed Mayellen, who was squirming. "Really." She put her hand on Burke's chest and a shiver ran down his spine. "It's just a fender-bender, only—those police! It took forever!" She rubbed her forehead against Mayellen's. "But how are you, pumpkin? How was your night? Was the wait bad?" Turning to Burke, she said, "Why are you so sweaty?"

For a second the carnival sounds grew large. A car screeched out of the lot. Mayellen lay her head against her mother's neck, eyeing Burke.

"Daddy ran all over," Mayellen said. "He thought you were lost."

"He did, did he?" Sandra said.

Burke, who'd been ready to tell the truth—about being late, and trying to win the bottle toss, and Mayellen sleeping on the ground in front of the booth—looked off down the midway.

"Mayellen," he said finally.

Sandra bounced Mayellen on her hip. "What is it, pumpkin? Huh?"

"Look what daddy won!" she said, and pointed to the monkey there on the bench.

The Luck at Lord Fletcher's

It was to be an evening of fun, Paula's father had said, nothing fancy, just fun, but now, primping her hair in the mirror—straightening the heavy barrette in back—she wondered. Ray, behind her at the dresser, whistled tunelessly, lifting one mismatched pair of socks after another.

"Do you have to do that?" she asked.

"What?" he said.

"Whistle."

Immediately Ray stopped whistling and began humming.

"That, too," Paula said.

There, the earrings did work after all. She turned her head from side to side. Her father wouldn't like it—too *something*, he'd say, which made Paula smile. Ray had gotten her the earrings, cheerful green shamrocks, in Dublin.

"He isn't that bad," Ray said, standing behind her, kissing her neck.

"You don't know him as well as I do," Paula said.

Ray made a face behind her, a long, sad, serious face. Paula laughed, pushing him away.

"Don't, *please*. You don't know how serious it is. And you have to pick up the check tonight, no matter what. You won't let it go, *whatever* he does. I mean absolutely not, for any reason. Okay?"

"I'll think of something," Ray said.

"Like last time?"

The last time Paula's father had excused himself from the table, only to return moments later grinning conspicuously and folding the check into his breast pocket. "I like your perfume," Ray said. He bit Paula on the neck.

"Stop, you'll make marks," she laughed.

In the car, Ray driving, Paula was thinking about her father, her hands clenched in her lap. As usual, he'd called late in the week, asking them to Lord Fletcher's on Lake Minnetonka, a boozy, upper crust hangout for those who had boats docked on the south shore, as did Paula's father. Frank, a successful stock broker, always called late, and in an almost proprietary way, as if Paula and Ray never had other plans. And, too, she thought now, why couldn't he have invited them to The Blue Heron, downtown? Something less... exclusive.

Paula reached over and straightened Ray's tie, flattened the lapels of his jacket.

"Hey, there," Ray said.

"We've got to get you a new sportcoat."

"Right." The look on Ray's face darkened a second, and then he smiled.

Ray was a photographer. He had recently done layouts for *National Geographic* and *Life* magazines, and had a few more projects in the works, the biggest of which Paula feared he might lose. He'd spent all those months away in Ireland, and now, they were waiting for final approval of Ray's photographs for a newspaper travel feature. So she was wearing the shamrock earrings. For luck.

"You don't like my threads?" Ray asked.

Paula rolled her eyes. On any other occasion the jacket would have been fine. But not for an outing with her father, at Lord Fletcher's. This, in part, was what angered Paula, that her father seemed to engineer these evenings to a specific effect, and always the deadly, end of the evening line he delivered, standing—*I know your ship is yet to come in, so*—

"Do you have enough money with you?"

"We could fly your father to the North Pole tonight if we wanted," Ray said.

The road curved through tall, dark pines, the night coming on. Ray was whistling again, a little Vivaldi. Paula studied him at the wheel. Just looking at him made her smile. He'd broken his nose in some boyhood fight and it was flattened a bit to one side. He had heavy brows, and a strong jaw, and a boyish smile.

Ray squeezed her knee. "You're thinking about your father," he said. "I can tell." He hunched over the wheel, his face clownishly twisted into a grimace. "*If he so much as mentions my mother I'll scream, I really will, I promise*," Ray teased.

Paula sighed. "Enough."

"What, still sad you didn't marry that guy your old man had you hooked up with?"

Paula, years back, had dated an investment banker named Ted Milton, whose idea of a good time had been to watch market returns on cable television.

Paula laughed.

.

But it was not so funny at Lord Fletcher's, at the bar, waiting for her father. The barrette she'd put in her hair felt cheap now, it was pewter, not silver, and she longed to remove the earrings. Shamrocks! What had she been thinking? Everywhere around her were women in the most exquisite outfits, most of them hand-tailored, the men, almost as if in uniform, in three piece navy blue or gray. From all corners of Lord Fletcher's diamonds glittered. And, too, now the mirror behind the bar was making accusations.

She could be, it said: *more striking, prettier, more....* Paula frowned.

Her father in the picture, suddenly everything seemed shabby. The car Ray had bought from another photographer, the small condominium in the Uptown area, Ray's work abroad, knit together out of assignments that always materialized, but came sporadically. Even her bakery.

"This is Tom Burke," Ray said, introducing Paula to a bespectacled older man on his left. They were laughing about something or another.

The two shook hands.

"Lovely to meet you," Tom said, and added a bit drunkenly, "And you're lovely too."

Paula turned her back on him.

Paula's father, Frank, marched to the bar, black tie, straight and tall and effective looking, and very late. Paula's heart sank at the sight of him. Beside her, Ray, in his worn Harris tweed, had begun to look, as usual, too comfortable. Ray followed Frank to the table, Paula trailing behind.

After a fluster of demands, and curt requests of the waiter, all Frank's doing, the table was set, a martini for Frank, a beer for Ray, a Chablis for Paula.

"Avoid the seafood," Frank said, smiling, and lifting his menu.

Paula, hearing it, thought she would die. Just like that, her father had seized control of the evening, down to the last detail.

"So," Frank said. "Tell me all about the little business—

Which was Paula's bakery, Griffin and Clarke, just off 57th and Nicollet. As if asked to sing on demand, she detailed the readings they'd had recently, to bring in customers, college kids most of them; the renovation on the second floor; the new bakery goods—all excellent and fresh, and put together by Jean, their French pastry chef (she didn't mention he was an incorrigible drunk); the line of exotic teas and coffee that had been a hit.

"So," she said, clasping her hands, "We're off and running."

Paula's father nodded. "Great," he said.

He had been concerned, earlier, when Ray and Paula described the location. That's donut territory, he'd said, not... *brioche folks.* Don't you think?

Still, the shop was beautiful, had good northern exposure, was of attractive red brick, was light and spacious and, in a word, *lovely*, something Paula had always wanted.

"And you, Ray? How's show biz?" Frank asked.

"I just shoot pictures," Ray replied. "Sell a few here and there."

While the two discussed politics, teased each other, Paula slumped in her chair.

She had envisioned, in the bedroom, dressing, some change in the usual protocol, some perhaps subtle effect she or Ray might have on her father's not too subtle directorial behavior. But here, at Lord Fletcher's, her father was at his most charming, and even Ray had succumbed to it.

Sipping his second martini, with a broad smile, Frank, needled Ray for details:

"How far can you see with one of those big telephoto lenses? You ever see something, you know, *racy*?"

In a voice thick with good will and possibility, he asked, had Ray ever thought of taking some pictures on the sly? Didn't photographers commonly sell pictures to *The Enquirer*, or *The Star* for astronomical sums? How about that? He could shoot for the *Enquirer* and still do this... third world stuff when he had time, Frank said, and dug into his beef burgundy with tremendous relish.

"That would be fun, wouldn't it, gumshoeing around, snapping pictures for the *Enquirer*?"

"Dad," Paula said.

The waiter brought the dessert menu and Frank insisted they order cheesecake. Frank, chewing, pointed his fork at Ray across the table.

"Paula tells me you've got something big on the horizon?"

Ray looked suddenly—*impish*—yes, that was it, Paula thought.

"I was going to tell you later," Ray said, turning to Paula and smiling, "but—" he hammered his fingers on the table top, a kind of drum roll "—I got the *Times* piece! Ten-pager, three color. The works! What do you say? Is that great, or what?"

Paula beamed.

"Congratulations," Frank said, lifting his glass.

They enthused over the extraordinary articles they'd seen in the *Times Magazine* over the years. The possibilities for more, there, or in other, also well known, magazines.

"And what does something like that pay?" Frank asked. "That's top drawer, isn't it?"

Ray named the price the *Times* had agreed to, and that, Paula knew, he'd gotten only after some hard negotiation. Be tough, she'd told him; and here he'd done it.

"It's that piece on Dublin," Paula said, and pointed to her earrings.

Frank nodded, then cocked his head to one side, calculating.

"Hey, that's great, Ray. Really great." Frank tossed down the last of his martini. "What—you only have to sell, ten... fifteen a year like that?"

Paula, caught off guard, dropped her fork, coughed into her napkin. She cut a look across the table at Ray, who, grinning affably, was not about to explain anything to Frank, not now, and not later. Alfred Eisenstaedt hadn't placed ten pieces a year, not in the *Times*, but it would be rude to say it.

Frank looked askance at Ray, then Paula. Both of them had gone back to their dinners.

The upset done with, Frank lifted the fudge frosting from the top of his cheesecake and cut it into small, rectangular wedges. He ate each with appreciative, mincing bites. Frank loved cheesecake. Paula and Ray watched, fascinated.

"Is something wrong?" Frank asked, and set his fork beside his plate.

And the strange thing was, Paula thought, he meant it. He didn't understand the silence. Ray, across the table, was eating his dinner, privately amused. Later, Paula knew, he would say, wasn't that *grand theater*? Isn't your old man a *classic*?

"Did I miss something?" Frank demanded.

"No," Paula said, "everything's fine," and set her hand over her father's.

Her feelings ran to something not unlike pity, even though the tough, hard face Frank was showing them now she'd seen far too much of growing up. Paula's mother had divorced him some time ago for just this reason. Nothing gets through to him, Paula's mother had told her, heartbroken, *nothing*.

·

A jazz band played and the evening went on. The music of Paul Whiteman in the background, Ray was discussing the greens of Ireland. He pointed to Paula's earrings, Just that color. Mmmm, Frank said, but aren't those a little? I don't know—*Green*, Paula said, and giving it up, said, Ray would take her with him, to see the small villages, the warm pubs, the coasts shrouded in fog.

She enthused over the old books she'd find, the antiques, for the bakery. And like that, the evening came alive again. The table was awash in good feeling. At one point, Ray even put his arm around Paula's father's shoulders, tugging at him.

"Hey, lighten up," he said.

"I am light," Frank said, joking.

Ray put a beer in front of him. "Drink up," he said. "You were telling us about Fletcher's back in the Fifties. When it was really big and grand and there was no place for riffraff around here."

"Was I?" Frank asked.

.

It was late, and now there was little left to be said: the musicians had gone on break. The bus boys were dodging from table to table, whisking away the dinner finery, and the younger night crowd had come in, hustling.

Paula was waiting. She had earlier resigned herself to her father's final, authoritative act of standing, so it came as no surprise when he did, in that tall and well-dressed and affable way of his. But now, Ray was standing too, catching the check at exactly the moment Frank did, so that they were both holding the check as if in a tug-of-war. Now Paula couldn't bring herself to say what she'd intended to say, It's on us, our treat, our turn.

"*I'll* take that," Frank said, winking, then pulling at the check.

"No, *I'll* get it," Ray said, grinning and pulling back.

The others in the restaurant turned to watch. It was an odd little scene:

Paula, lovely, but distressed, held a hand to her mouth, the cheerful shamrocks dangling from her ears. The two men in front of her tugged at the check, seesawing over the table. Around them, polite conversation ceased, and the rattle of clean-up seemed louder for it.

"All right," Paula's father said, and really pulled now.

"Ray," Paula said, turning to him, the tone of her voice suggesting what they agreed on earlier. Her heart hammered wildly in her chest.

Ray's grin broadened; he blinked.

"Enough," Frank said, and gave another tug in his direction, "Come on. What's up?"

Suddenly, Ray bent over the table and, with his free hand motioning Paula's father closer, dipped and kissed the back of Frank's hand.

Frank snapped his hand back. Ray boyishly waved the check over his head.

"I don't know what to say," Frank said.

"Just '*thanks*,' should do it," Ray said, cheerfully, and bustled off to the desk.

Paula dug in her purse, what for she couldn't think. When she glanced up, her father shrugged so as to settle his dinner jacket over his shoulders. He was working himself up to say something, but nothing came, and a long, awkward minute passed. He looked at the back of his hand, where Ray had kissed it.

Paula, her eyes on her father, waited for him to put on that million kilowatt smile, to throw his shoulders back and make some coarse joke.

"Lucky I didn't kiss him back," Frank chuckled and lifted his fist. "Right?"

He'd fixed his eyes on Ray, who was talking with someone at the door. Now, Frank wouldn't budge with Ray there waiting. He shifted his weight slightly and gripped the back of his chair.

Something in his discomfort caught in Paula's throat. A flame. A stab of something. A glimmer. She'd expected only to feel elated, but here was this loss now, too. Frank was gritting his teeth against it. At his chair, he bent at the waist, older somehow. Alone. And when the moment stretched unbearably, Paula said,

"Oh, Daddy," which she hadn't said in years, and taking his arm, more than a little sadly led him out of Lord Fletcher's.

Return

San Marco in Spring

The holidays, let me tell you, make me uneasy.

Like these gifts I get, especially from family, many of them nothing more than not so subtle hints or manipulations. The calendar I received express mail (late) from my mother yesterday, for example. There, at the post slot over my kitchen counter, I regard her gift as I might a snake, on the cover the Grand Canal in all its splendor—palaces and monuments and gaily colored banners waving in a breeze.

My mother lives in Venice now, off the Piazza San Marco, so in the calendar, I know, is a suggestion I should visit.

She has been sending me these calendars for twenty years, and each year I tear the calendar in half, exactly where I stand, and drop the two halves into the waste basket under the sink.

But yesterday I didn't do that. I turn the calendar over and glance at the pictures of Venice there. Of Vapporetto. Of the Accademia. Of the romantic and winding streets. Of buildings, Byzantine, Renaissance, and Gothic, otherworldly. Of revelers in the Carnevale. And before I can act to distance myself, I notice, at the bottom of the page, what appears to be some inspirational message, of the kind my father is still fond, but it is something else.

"*Of magic doors there is this: You do not see them, even as you are passing through,*" it read.

And without thinking, I clutch the calendar to my chest, this sudden stab of pain there, in it a memory so powerful my legs threaten to collapse under me, and I ask myself, again, if I did the right thing.

Always, I have thought, Yes, the house around me, and my husband at work, the children at school, but yesterday, poised to rend my mother's gift in two, I wondered, and doing so, recalled the time I'd passed through such a door one bright May morning in 1963.

.

We were at the breakfast table, and the bell rang, and all of us, my twin sisters, Lisle and Lisa, just nine, and my brother, Bobby, seven, looked up. My mother, at the stove in her blue robe, was making scrambled eggs.

"Well? Are you going to get it?" my father asked, rattling his newspaper.

My mother, brushing her hands on her robe, went out into the foyer. I jumped up to take the eggs from the range, where she'd left them. She'd been doing things like that the last year, lost in thoughts she didn't share with us. I waited at the stove, seconds that seemed like an eternity, to make my mother's having abandoned the eggs seem intentional, then followed her out.

In the foyer, she stood back of the door, seeming to collect herself.

A wash of yellow light came through the picture window to the right, transforming that small room into a setting out of a Dutch painting: the cat dish scarlet over ochre ceramic tiles, the shefalera nearly glowing, verdigris itself, and my mother in the middle of it, in her cobalt robe, a seeming vision.

And I thought, all was lost—if my mother opened the door. It was this look in her eyes, as if, at the stove, she'd decided something. On chance, perhaps, and now it had come knocking.

And here Lisle and Lisa, and Bobby, ran in behind me, and she opened the door, onto that late May morning:

Sweet smelling lilacs bloomed in our hedge, and a heavy scent of traffic came from down the block, promising motion, and travel, and adventure, in the air itself this fecund, hopeful *something*.

Only here, on the stoop between all that and us, stood a rather handsome man wearing a black suit, white shirt, and yellow tie. He had that dark, vulnerable Monty Clift look about him.

"Mrs. Jorgenson?" he asked, consulting the clipboard he'd lifted from his side.

My mother rolled her eyes. *Business.* How business bored her! Certainly she'd already gotten enough of it from my father. And here, I suppose, I breathed a sigh of relief, the spell broken—or so I thought—standing on my toes behind her.

"Irene," she said, glancing over her shoulder at me, a note of exasperation in her voice, and I stepped off to the side.

I had just turned twelve a few months before, and this mystery of men and women was of great interest to me now, but here I'd gone and embarrassed myself.

But the salesman cleared his throat now, embarrassed too. He'd blushed badly, and was trying to hop back on that departing train of his once well-oiled sales spiel, and wasn't having much success. Surely he hadn't expected to run into someone like my mother. She had modeled for J.C. Penny and Sears while at the university, and could still slip into that studied, haughty composure at will. People said she looked like Ingrid Bergman, though my mother was a more full-figured woman, you might say, and that, I think, was what the salesman was reacting to, that and my mother's intimidating silence.

"Mrs. Jorgenson," he said, squaring his shoulders, "my name is— (and I here I have to wait for his name to come to me, as I have so long suppressed my memory of it--) James Byron," he said, "and I'm from General Mills. We're conducting a series of tests in this area and—"

"Tell him we don't want any," my father shouted from the kitchen.

"It's an experiment of some sort," my mother called back. She held the door, craning her head around, an ear trained on the kitchen. Modeling, I could see that.

"Experiment?"

The salesman smiled. Bobby, and Lisle and Lisa, were crowding the door to see what it was all about, and I marshaled them away.

"Yes?" my father said, suddenly at the door with us.

Unlike my mother, my father was neither tall nor striking. But he had about him this unassailable boyish air, was both authoritarian and chipper, and I think that was what the salesman saw immediately. Crew cut, muscular arms, a broad, flat forehead and no-nonsense eyes. A doctor's eyes.

"You'd better make it good," my father said, and smiled.

The salesman swallowed hard, that color rising in his face again, caught out somehow. But, glancing up suddenly, he threw his winning pitch.

"Free cereal," he said. "About a hundred bucks worth."

My father squinted; the twins and Bobby giggled.

"Shhhh!" I said, trying to smooth things out, as if I really could have.

"You know, I was about to shut the door in your face," my father said. "So—*free?*"

He let that word hang. He put his big, thick-fingered hand proprietarily on my mother's shoulder. She smiled—queenly. Suddenly I was happy. But then realized my mother wasn't.

"So, what's the catch?" asked my father.

"No catch," the salesman replied, grinning, teeth as white as fine china. He opened his case, dug around in there, made a lot of noise. We were all happy for the distraction.

"Strawberries already in the cereal," he said. "A new marvel of food science—*freeze dried.* Only--" he held up an index finger "—from General Foods. You won't believe it." Handing my mother two unmarked boxes, he added, "You've just got to let us know how much you like us—" and he blushed again, "I mean, them when I come back. How's that for a deal?"

My mother, her voice pitched low, and sultry said, "Lovely."

.

Now, more than for any reason, I remember that week for the business with the salesman, and my mother's peculiar behavior at the door, because everything in our lives changed at their meeting. But, when I think on it, I remember that week, too, for the unusual, and especially warm weather; and for the odd sense of mystery over what had happened to our Easter Break trip to Florida—we just didn't go. And I remember that week for what we saw on T.V.—the twins, and Bobby, and my mother and I—sitting evenings my father was working late in front of our Zenith, the whole world in flux, seeming near bursting.

In Birmingham, Black children, well-dressed and with blank looks on their faces, marched into a school past screaming bigots. A fire in a Consolidated Coal Company mine killed seventy men, who we saw stacked in bags on flatbed trucks. Gordon "Gordo" Cooper circled the planet in Faith 7. "Boy, oh boy, is it ever clear up here," he said, and when his automated guidance system failed, he caught the nation's attention as we watched John Glenn at Mission Control guide him to a perfect splash landing.

It was a roller coaster ride that week, one moment cheers and applause, the next, tragedy.

And through it all, curled on one end of the sofa, my mother plucked at the cushions until the nubbly purple fabric came undone.

I worried about her. She burned another dinner, and we threw together something to replace it. And she was fighting with my father again. We could hear them nights, their voices low when they thought we were sleeping.

"That's enough disaster for today," I'd tell her, standing to turn the set off.

"Irene," my mother would threaten, and the Twins, and Bobby would shout, "Don't!"

So I didn't, not until Saturday of that week, a cold, rainy evening.

We'd gotten the usual disasters, and as a cap, or epilogue of sorts, Walter Cronkite gave us the news of "Yetta" Wallenda's death. Walter detailed her life and work with the Ringling Brothers Circus, her world famous tightrope balancing act, and following was the footage of Yetta's fall, fifty feet or so, her body hitting the dirt floor with such force and speed they showed it three times, just so we wouldn't miss it.

"Her life was one of art skirting the borderline of eternity," Walter said in that inimitable, baleful voice of his.

There on the couch, my mother burst into tears, cried so hard she couldn't catch her breath. I ushered the Twins and Bobby to their rooms, then called our father at his clinic.

Home from work, he went downstairs, spoke to my mother in a low, soothing voice.

"She'll be fine," he told me at the door into my room, but she cried later that night, too.

At the breakfast table the following morning, though, my mother, with a big, conciliatory smile, poured orange juice for Bobby, kissed Lisle and Lisa on the cheek, and straightened the barrette in my hair. We all chewed vacantly, making as if we were the Nelsons or the Cleavers. The cereal was awful.

"Pretty good, huh?" my father said, turning the yellow box as if to read it. "I mean the fruit."

Bobby, to my right, was spitting out the strawberries (or I should say what the cereal company was passing off as strawberries) when my father wasn't watching. Lyle and Lisa swallowed them whole. I was sitting on the edge of my chair, hoping they didn't choke. I rehearsed what I would do if they did.

"Taste is good," said my father.

"Yes," I agreed.

My mother nodded. "But I think they could do something with the texture, don't you?"

"Oh, I don't know," I said, but taking my cue, went on from there, held court on those strawberries. I was, after all, on my mother's side.

"Slimy, as a description of these strawberries, would be an understatement," I contended.

"Could you be more specific?" my father asked.

I thought for a minute, then answered, and when the salesman came with the second set of boxes, I told him exactly what I had my father, at seven-fifteen A.M., the screen door between us, and my mother batting her eyelashes and behaving strangely again.

"Unctuous, vile-smelling clots of sour putrescence," I told the salesman.

"You didn't like the size or texture?" he said.

"Limaceous," I replied.

"I'm sorry—what?"

"Slug-like," I said with some pride.

I felt my father's large, muscular hand on the back of my neck.

"She likes to kid around," he said, squeezing a little, "play with big words. Don't worry. She doesn't understand any of it."

I smiled. My mother smiled. Lisle and Lisa and Bobby smiled.

The salesman handed my mother two questionnaires.

"For the lady of the house," he said, chuckling. "I'll pick them up next time around." And pulling a new box of cereal from his sample case, he added, "Now—you *won't believe these*!"

My mother said she would try to, and with a wink the salesman was gone, and then my mother, and Lisle and Lisa and Bobby, and I went back into the kitchen. I could tell my mother was unhappy, but it wasn't about the cereal. I knew that much.

"I feel like a lab rat," I said.

My father tore the top off one of the new boxes. He held up some thin, withered thing, and popped it into his mouth. He chewed thoughtfully, sniffing.

"Hmmm..."

"It might help to know what this stuff is to see if we like it," I said. "I mean—for instance—If I'd known those strawberries were really weasels' hearts—"

"Cut it out, Reenie," my father said.

"I don't see why we have to eat this stuff," I complained.

"Hey, it isn't so bad, is it?" he said. "Is it Irene?"

To be fair to my father, I must say, looking back on that time, we were all engaged in some grand experiment, down to the last breathing soul. That Science (whipped up by a faceless "they") would solve all the world's problems was a notion heralded everywhere, but especially in the newspapers of the time. *Sea Harvest Will End World Hunger!* the headlines read. *Amazing new Fabric Never Fades!* (but was it ever scratchy and did it make you sweat!) *Science Unlocks the Secret of the Atom! Wonder Pill Cures Depression!* Each week brought some new so-called "wonder." So why not food, too?

My father believed all that.

"Just use your old noggin," he'd say, "and you can figure it out."

It drove my mother nuts, his saying it. Especially the way he said it, as if he'd gotten the world's confusion behind him once and for all. It was a posture men assumed back then, jaunty, in control, in it a dapper insouciance. For implicit in the thinking of that time was a belief in some all encompassing grand design, one which could be gotten at and understood. One writer, I recall, compared the acquisition of this knowledge to tracing one's finger down and into the chambered shell of a nautilus, there reaching some one, finite end.

And nowhere was this belief more strongly present than in the *Tribune's Parade of Homes* magazine supplement. There, in three color spreads, miles and miles of unblemished carpet beckoned like warm Florida beaches, windows sparkled, fires crackled reassuringly in rustic fireplaces, in it, all meaningful and harmonious order, and light, and reason.

.

That things weren't like that in our house, and never had been, was a big disappointment to my father, I think—that our house, instead of seeming like some well-ruled and tiny monarchy, was at best some Wild Kingdom.

In our house, plants—my mother had them everywhere—climbed out of stands and up makeshift trellises, spilled from terra cotta pots, burst into bloom on windowsills. Sports gear, Bobby's bats and baseballs and gloves, and the twins jump ropes and roller skates, and my intaglio plates and stones were scattered from one end of the house to the other, alongside jackets and scarves, and boots and shoes for all kinds of weather, and always there was a flurry of paper, school paper, and Bobby's paper airplanes, and the rough paper which my mother had us drawing on, and painting on, and everywhere, too, were art books, say on Matisse, or Rodin, or Van Gogh, the books set open, their spines broken, on the sofa, or balanced on the Hi Fi, or perched on the piano, to inspire us.

When my father pointed out my mother's treating the books that way broke their spines, my mother remarked that it made the books easier to open.

After all, she said, that's what books were for, weren't they? To open, and look at?

But, even if the constant mess in the house was some sore point between them, it was the plants that got them really fighting.

One rainy Sunday, months after the salesman had first stopped by, my mother got an ornamental orange tree and a grow light. My father, home from errands, kicked at the soil in the carpet around the planter.

"Why didn't you vacuum this up?" he asked.

"I was out shopping," she told him.

This I doubted, as she'd gotten all the groceries earlier in the week. And I suspect now my father did as well.

That was the month of the "blueberry" cereal. Monty, as we'd gotten to calling him, had stopped by after we'd had time to "test" it, with a new set of boxes and questionnaires. His hand, I'd noticed, when he'd given the questionnaires to my mother, had rested on hers a moment, the space of a breath.

I think my father noticed that too, as after that morning, he was inclined to fight with my mother, as he did over the ornamental orange tree.

"I don't understand why you go to all the trouble," he said that afternoon. "Why don't we just get plastic plants? You don't have to mess with them."

My mother grinned, something awful in it.

"Fine," she said.

The following morning she dumped her plants—all of them, even her cactuses—in a heap in the back yard. I remember having tried to put the plants back into their pots, but she came out in the middle of it and hacked the plants to bits with a hoe.

I think my mother, when my father was around, was a lot like her plants had been, cramped for space (if given any at all). But when my father left mornings, she blossomed. She put on Edith Piaf, and we all sang along with her, to *T'Es Beau, Tu Sais*, and *La Vie En Rose*, and *La Goualante De Pauvre Jean*, and we danced in the living room, even Bobby. She'd show us some complicated steps, then leave us to "perfect them" while she drank from the fancy bottles in the kitchen cupboards.

When she returned, she swirled us in circles—*Shooting Stars*, she called it—until we all tumbled to the soft, wool-smelling carpet. Some mornings, her jubilation was such that, we would have been afraid, but we were all having such a wonderful time.

But then, on one such manic morning something did happen.

My father had bought a new Chrysler, a convertible, and after the Piaf and a few turns from the bottle, my mother got us into the car to go for a drive. The car was a 300, powerful and sleek, my father's baby—he left the gray, Ford Fairlane for my mother to drive. But this morning, my mother got us into "Daddy's Rocket," and with the top down and a scarf wrapped around her head, out on the road, my mother raced the motor and made the tires squeal turning sharply around corners.

We all thought this was great fun, until, headed back to the house, we heard a horn behind us.

A fussy-looking gent in a tweed cap, a pipe clamped in his yellowed teeth, pulled up alongside. He was driving some sleek sports car, and nodded to my mother with a certain condescension and, with a stiff-necked self-assurance, moved to pass.

"I'll be goddamned!" my mother said, and sent that big Chrysler shooting forward.

Tweedy in the car to our side shot forward too, and like that we were racing, bumper to bumper, my mother bent low over the wheel.

Just short of the cloverleaf, Tweedy made one last attempt to pass. It was pure madness.

"Over my *dead body*," my mother said, and she kicked the accelerator to the floor, and that Chrysler seemed to cough, and as if rearing, catapulted ahead, passing the sports car and highsiding so badly in the cloverleaf we went up on two wheels.

Lisle and Lisa screamed. Bobby, white-faced, gripped the handle in the back door. I braced my feet against the floor mat. But what scared me most was my mother's laughter, high, exuberant, triumphant.

"We sure showed the old fart, didn't we?!" she shouted. "Didn't we now?!"

But in the garage, and out of the car, the door automatically closing, my mother turned to us, suddenly in tears.

"We won't tell," I said. "We promise."

And when we saw that made her smile, we rushed toward her, and she gathered us into her arms, sobbing, and smelling of Chanel, which I still can't smell without remembering.

"Let's go inside," I said, and we did that.

.

Yet, even if there were a number of incidents elsewhere—out on the highway in the car; or at the grocery store ("Why should I take your green stamps?" my mother asked a cashier one afternoon. "What are they good for but fifth rate merchandise I could get cheaper at any corner retailers? Can you answer me *that*?)—somehow things always got worked out in the house.

The house this, the house that. By that time, my mother had gone on some vaguely-defined campaign to reassert her tastes at home, and our house looked like some long-standing argument. She'd had Victorian shutters hung over the blue vinyl siding. Her flowers and antiques reposed now alongside my father's chrome and glass.

I called the house "eclectic." My mother called it "schizophrenic." But it was my father's opinion, in our house, which was the deciding one.

"An embarrassment," he called the house, his complaint having in it a certain indignation, as if the disorder were a violation of some sacred trust.

But he was right. When cupboards were opened, pots and pans in no order whatsoever fell clattering to the floor. The refrigerator had oranges in it in fuzzy green jackets. And the freezer in the garage was full of the dead birds my mother collected from below the picture window on the west side of the house. A big mirror when the sun was bright, the picture window attracted all kinds—orioles, cardinals, wrens, jays. Birds flew headlong into that window. My mother wanted to put something up to stop them, but was thwarted by my father, who said hanging strips of cloth, as my mother suggested, would make the living room seem like a cage. So, she collected the beautiful, but dead, birds in the freezer, claiming some day she'd give them to a taxidermist.

When my father, looking for the ice cream out there one afternoon, complained, "Jesus, just what we need, another pile of... what is this, Reenie?" I replied, cannily, "Disorder. All systems tend toward disorder, unless acted upon, right? You taught me that."

"Right," my father replied, and smiling winningly, he said, "and guess who's going to act upon this one?"

Trapped again, I thought.

We all were. But most of all my mother, because she'd known another life. My mother could dance to Piaf, drive as aggressively as any man, argued nights with my father—"I like that your mother's got spunk," he told me—but when we were together, all six of us, she was quiet, seemingly overwhelmed, and when coerced by my father, might laugh, but then a little hysterically.

Still, sometimes I didn't know who was crazier, our mother or—

I have already said my father was neither tall nor striking. But he was handsome, and that's what must have first attracted my mother.

He was boyish, energetic, and brazenly optimistic. He pulled you right into that big old American Dream of his, that Heratio Algier dream.

He was going to put a man on the moon—why, *his* taxes were doing that already. (I don't think it ever occurred to him that *his* tax dollars were also threatening to blow us all to kingdom come.) *His* company had built row upon row of affordable apartment houses, first come, first serve! (So what if the places looked like WWII pillboxes or housing for the criminally insane. Fewer windows meant they were easier to heat, my father said.)

He even tied his wingtips with bravado, two colors, black or brown.

One evening, buoyed up by some recent success, my father said, "We've built ourselves a nice little family, haven't we?!"

We were all sitting around the kitchen table at dinner. We all bent over our plates.

"Sure have," I replied, finally, suspecting something was up, and he smiled that boyish smile at us, a beacon of reason, possibility, and good will.

.

I remember that dinner, because the following Saturday morning, in my father's absence, my mother delivered a speech of sorts at the kitchen table, one I knew immediately was not her own. Just then she had an almost fanatical glitter in her eyes, of the kind you might imagine seeing in a convert to say, Pentecostalism, or the Krishnas.

"We're going to run this house like a ship from now on," she said. She attempted then to smile something like my father, but couldn't quite pull it off, and grimaced, really, instead.

"But this *isn't* a ship," Lisle whined, and Lisa nodded.

Bobby, considering the possibilities of this plan, as they might benefit him, shouted enthusiastically, "I get to be captain!"

At that, my mother rose to her full, intimidating height over the table. "Will you *let me finish*?" she said.

I thwocked Bobby's head lightly, gave the Twins a threatening stare. My mother nodded, thanking me, then gathered herself up and said,

"It has come to my attention that—"

And there she lost us, dictating from a crumpled sheet of paper she took from her pocket. Chores, done correctly and on time. Punctual behavior. A chain of command, our father playing a kind of admiral to our mother's captain. And as she went on, she began to slump, until she lay her head on the table, saying nothing.

Which was terrifying.

So I commandeered the vacuum cleaner, and Lisle and Lisa attacked dust and dirt and smudgy windows. Bobby took his post at the sink, washing dishes (a job he did as poorly as possible, knowing my father—stickler for sanitary flatware that he was—would take one look between the tines of the forks and reinstate Lisle and Lisa, and myself, as dishwashers).

While we were working, our mother locked herself in her bedroom and cried, and it took our father, back from his clinic, to calm her down. They must have come to some agreement in that room because, after that, our Saturday morning cleaning was followed by boozy grocery sprees, in which we bought fresh Alaska salmon, and French vanilla ice cream, and thick juicy steaks, Portobello mushrooms, jars of artichoke hearts in olive oil, and bricks of exotic cheeses.

And when we *didn't* go shopping with her?

"Voila!" she'd call out, stumbling from the convertible, even though, by then, it was only forty degrees out, and for sensible people, too cold to have the top down, no matter what you wore on your head.

And bribed like that, we tried.

·

A month went by, the new order surviving a shaky start through my mother's concerted efforts. The house looked better, but in the living room, where we never went then, so as not to mess things up, there was a sour, stuffy feeling. It was like that in much of the house. And our mother tippled more often, and a lift home from school was a sure rollercoaster ride.

T.V. was regulated, a dangerous influence.

My father's clinic took on new patients and business was good, but his spirits terrible, my father overworked and irritable when he returned from a day at the clinic.

"Why hasn't this garbage been taken out, Bobby?" he'd shout, stepping through the door. "What's this doing here, Irene?"

And too impatient to wait for my mother to heat whatever she'd saved of our dinner for him, he'd reach into the cupboard and pull down one of those boxes of nifty cereal.

We had quite a collection by that time—so many boxes we'd stopped trying to figure out what was in them.

Prune Delight, I'd called this last set: dark, fruit-filled oat confections that stuck between your teeth where you could not only see them all day, but you could taste them as well. The flavor, as with the other cereals, they hadn't yet perfected.

Monty made his usual stop, now always on the 30th. When he stood at the door, my mother's eyes flashed. Now he wore a cranberry beret, and some jacket or another that put one in mind of painters, and he'd had his car, a French make I'd never heard of, repainted a dark, cobalt blue—my mother's favorite color.

My mother, there at the door, positively beamed at him and, for the first time, I couldn't think of him derisively as "Monty," anymore—this... *James Byron*.

Who, somehow, had insinuated himself on us, on my mother, it seemed.

She'd told us things about "Jim": That he was a student over at the university, a Ph.D. candidate in art history. And that he was saving money to study abroad the coming year. When I asked her how she knew these things, she'd replied,

"Oh, I called to be sure he was working for the cereal company," she said.

"There's no phone number on any of these boxes," I replied, and in a voice that sent a chill up my back, she told me,

"*Information*, Reenie. Don't forget, there are always ways to do things. They might not be your father's, but there are *ways*."

"So, how was this last sample?" Jim asked now.

While I studied Jim, standing there on our stoop, my father screwed his face up, as if perplexed. He was genuinely curious.

"Was that a touch of licorice in there?"

"Can't say," Jim said.

"You can say any old damn thing you want to," my father shot back, bristling. "What, the company own you? You don't have any *spine*, or what?"

It was a criticism we'd all heard directed at ourselves at one time or another.

"*Ae-nis*," my mother said, pronouncing the word with a long initial vowel. "I hadn't thought of that," she said. "How interesting."

We all stood there, stunned.

"That's ann-is," my father said, correcting her.

"That's what I said," said my mother.

.

I remember that interaction particularly, because that day Jim brought the last box of experimental cereal we sampled (freeze dried peach halves like ears lolling in sorghum biscuits), but also because, days later, my mother assembled us in my room. It was snowing heavily outside, and now more was on the way.

"A blizzard!" my mother said, as if just thrilled.

She had been depressed, holed up in her room recently, but now she had that glassy-eyed animation she'd had the day she nearly rolled the car. She'd teased her hair back from her forehead and had on a zebra-striped dress and black high heels, as if she were planning on going somewhere. She spun lightly on her feet, to show off the billow of the dress.

I got Lisle and Lisa, and Bobby, to sit on my bed, while my mother dug through a big, serious looking plastic bag. At the top of it was written, *Schmidt Inc.*, and below that, under dancing, animated notes, was a second line of print which read: *The World is in Love with Music!*

I got a sinking feeling in the pit of my stomach. There was something peculiar in the way my mother was handling whatever it was in that bag, and I was reminded of the time she'd told us we were going to run the house like a ship, what Lisle and Lisa and I'd since called her *Invasion of the Body Snatchers* day.

"Ta da!" she said, suddenly straightening, her shoulders squared and eyes aflash. In each hand she held sheet music, flourished like a Japanese fan.

"You liked *The Sound of Music*, didn't you?" she demanded.

The four of us stared. What, after all, did that have to do with sheet music?

"It was wonderful," I said. (Already my underarms were making moons of nervous sweat in my shirt.)

We had all gone to *The Sound of Music* earlier that year, had loved the opening sequence, Julie Andrews on that mountaintop, singing for all the world. I know that film now for what it is, pure treacle. But back then I'd found myself drawn into it, the singing, hikes in the mountains, dress balls, the drama in which the heroine and her trusts, children like ourselves (sort of), defeated evil Nazis to escape into the mountains. Even the chaste, sexless love scenes I found utterly romantic. I swooned at them.

"And it all really happened," my mother said. "Did you know that?" She'd stooped to address Lisle and Lisa and Bobby, holding a book, something about the von Trapp family. "And *that's* what *we're* going to do!" she said. "Sing!"

That word, *Sing!* struck us all like some donging bell of doom. She might just as well have asked us to swim the English Channel.

"Sing?" Lisle said, timorous.

"Like... *how?*" Lisa said, twisting her legs anxiously in that way my mother so disliked.

My mother had grown so animated she was scaring Bobby, and now I sat beside him.

"I don't *want* to sing," Bobby protested.

"But it'll be fun," I said. I forced myself up from the bed, spinning, in what I thought was (at the time) a graceful, open-armed circle, like Julie Andrews had done on the mountaintop.

"*The hills are alive!*" I sang, scaring myself with my now high, reedy voice.

I pulled Bobby up from the bed, and Lisle and Lisa, swung them around with me. It was all very exciting, in an awful sort of way, but when my mother tried to quiet us, and brandished the sheets of music in our faces, it was just too much.

Lisle held her hand up to her mouth and laughed, and Lisa joined her.

"*Sing!*" my mother commanded.

Some time before, my father had gotten us to march circles around the kitchen banging pots and pans to John Philip Sousa marches he played on the hi fi, but this was something entirely different.

"*Stop it!*" I said to Lisle and Lisa, but it just made them laugh all the harder. And just at that moment, Bobby's wail cut through Lisa's laughter like a siren.

"All right!" my mother said, her eyes ablaze. "Into the car!"

"The car?" I said. "It's a *blizzard* out there."

Dark was coming on. I thought of calling our father, but, watched moment to moment, even using the bathroom, I didn't dare. We packed our bags in a rush, then got in the car, the big Chrysler, and my mother, without opening the garage door, started it.

Sure, just then, she meant to kill us, I sat in front, my mind racing. I thought of ways I could knock her out, none of them in the range of possible, and then the garage door groaned open, and she backed the car down the drive, the tires skreeking and crackling in the new snow, but that was little consolation.

"We'll drive north," my mother said. "Get out the maps, Irene."

I did as I was told. Lisle and Lisa and Bobby, behind me, stared holes in the back of my head. Save us, Irene, their silence said.

We drove like that, out of town through the snow, what seemed an eternity.

"I'm hungry," Bobby said.

He'd opened the bag on his lap and taken one of Jim Byron's boxes of cereal from it. He shook the box, the cereal making a dry rustling.

My mother slammed on the brakes, the car skidding across the road and bumping over a curb. She craned her head around to look over the front seat.

"What is *that*?" she demanded.

When she saw what Bobby had there, she shouted, "OUT OF THE CAR! You, Bobby! *OUT!*" as if his having brought the cereal were some unforgivable betrayal. We all sat facing the windshield, afraid to so much as glance in her direction. Finally, she tore the box from Bobby, heaved it from her open window, and skidded away.

"Where are we going?" I asked.

"Switzerland," she said, gripping the wheel.

.

At International Falls, we took a high sweeping bridge across to Canada. The inspector on the Canadian side told us the roads north out of Fort Francis were closed, because of the blizzard. They'd set up road blocks, he warned us. I remember shuddering at that. I was wearing a pair of patent leather pumps and a light jacket, my father's—it fit me like a dress, the arms hanging apelike. Lisle and Lisa and Bobby were no better off.

Just miles from the border, we stopped at a grocery store and my mother tried to buy a chicken and some bananas and the clerk wouldn't take her money—U.S. currency. I thought that might be the end of it. But no, fuelled with indignation now, among other things, she swung that big Chrysler away from the store, and where we met the first roadblock, she did what I'd been dreading she might all along.

"Out!" she shouted. "All of you! Get out!"

This time there was no dissuading her with stricken looks. We tumbled from the car, all four of us. I lined Lisle and Lisa and Bobby in front of me, got my arms around them the best I could. A bitter cold wind was blowing and it cut right through my jacket.

"They're coming!" my mother said, standing crazed in front of us.

It was around five by that time, the lights blinking on in the streets. At the side of the road, in the falling snow, I thought of my father.

Down in St. Paul, he would be wrapping things up for the day, ready to head home.

Suddenly all that efficiency and order and routine of his seemed more than desirable.

"You take them north," my mother said to me, pointing beyond the barricade.

"Over the mountains?" I asked, though there were no mountains.

"Yes," she said. "Can you do that?"

I tightened my arms around Bobby and the twins, trying not to cry. I was freezing. Already my toes were numb.

"I will," I said.

I remember, even then, having wanted to say something witty, because I'd always been able to amuse my mother, break her bad moods, something like, *We'll wait for you by the old clock tower in Zurich*, or *Don't forget the password, Liebchen*.

But instead I stood, facing north, holding onto Bobby and the twins, the snow, cold and granular as sand, rushing in my face.

"When it's safe to cross," my mother said, "I'll blink the lights three times."

I pulled my father's jacket tight around my neck. "Cross to where?"

My mother pointed into the woods out beyond the yellow roadblock, where the trees rose out of the snow in a long, dark line.

"The border," she said. She hugged us all, fiercely, her hands like claws on my back. Then she got in the car and threw it in reverse, spun it back a block.

We waited in the falling snow. I had an ache the size of a fist in my throat.

"I'm scared," Lisle said.

Bobby looked up at me and nodded.

"Shhhh," I said.

The car roared, came weaving toward us, the headlights blinking three times. I thought for a moment she was going to run us over, but propelled us across that icy, snow covered blacktop anyway, hoping she would see this last gesture for what it was:

A show of faith.

.

It was a long way back to the grocery store, and when we got there it was closed. With a pop bottle, I smashed through the tiny window in the front door, then undid the bolt. Inside, I called the police, explained where we were, and that our mother had dropped us off, and must have had some car trouble. From where I was standing, I could see drifts as high as the roofs of cars stretching into infinity.

"Don't panic," the officer said.

"Panic?" I replied.

.

She sent postcards, at the rate of four or five a week. I charted her progress on a map I put up in my room. By June of that year, a swatch of flagged pins stretched from Finland, where she'd first flown (Helsinki), to England, and across the channel to Blankenburg, Belgium, and into the Netherlands.

I flagged more pins, anticipating her travels.

Having a wonderful trip, she'd write on each card, underlining the word wonderful three times. And sometimes would follow a word salad, *Saw monument like no other and paintings you couldn't believe how beautiful in the old city when the morning light shines*, or something like that, followed by, *Love, Genie.*

Lisle and Lisa and Bobby and I shared the cards. We kept them in my mother's jewelry box, which she'd emptied, once diamonds in it, and now too many cards there to fit, so we numbered them and put them in a shoe box.

"What kind of name is Rotterdam?" Bobby asked.

"Hell if I know," I said.

"You're not supposed to swear," Lisle said.

I considered the utility of what Lisle was asking of me.

"No more swearing," my father had said, his decree coming hard on the heels of our great trek through the Schwartzwald to the cozy hutte (the store) high in the Alps, where soon after we were captured by the Nazis—or should I say *Nazi?*

"Shit," I said, "I'll swear when I fucking want to."

Bobby smiled. "So where's she going now?" he asked, and I told him the truth.

No one knew for certain.

But it was a point of some contention between my father and my mother's family, anyway, where our, now labeled *non compos mentis*, mother was going. My father, in his usual, scientific fashion, argued for *institutionalization* (the funny farm, I told the twins and Bobby), were he able to find her and bring her home, my mother's sister and two brothers arguing vehemently against that, claiming my mother, were he to have her committed, would be unfit for anything.

"It would be terribly unfair to her, Roger," they said, "her condition doesn't warrant that."

So, nights they argued what should be done, after they had sent us away, confining us to the basement and table tennis, where I got my mother's hope chest out from under the clothes hamper, and with the help of Lisle and Lisa and Bobby, slid it under the big heating vent that opened onto the dining room.

I had a mouse's-eye-view from the vent, saw things from a new, and shocking angle. My aunt Louise's swollen calves, encased in the finest peach silk, and pointed satin heels (she wasn't quite as stunning as my mother, but this was actually to her advantage, it turned out, as men were not so intimidated by her); uncles Arthur and Ted's identical, pressed black slacks, black socks and shoes, nervous hands on knee caps, my mother's siblings having worked out a subtle communication of kicks and jabs.

It was like watching sign language for the deaf.

Finally, they decided it would be best to wait until Genevieve, as they called my mother, "took root" somewhere—at which time, my father, and Lisle and Lisa, and Bobby and I would all fly over and tempt her home—to a "normal life" my father added, which inspired Louise to give Arthur and Ted, each, a meaningful jab under the table.

And like that we waited. The cards continued to find our mailbox almost daily, all of them from the Rhine now—pleasure boats and cruises, scenic overlooks, each having some obscure postmark, my pins and their flags bristling in my map just south of Stuttgart.

So it came as some shock when, one Friday afternoon, my father arrived home early, telling us to pack, we'd be flying to Paris.

"*Paris?*" I asked.

"Reenie," he said, "she's been in France all this time, don't ask me to explain. Just get ready."

I bolted upstairs, but standing in front of my map, I felt the first stirrings of some resistance, struck by the thought my mother, given her months' long ruse with the postcards, *hadn't wanted* to be found.

"You'll be ready," my father called up to me, and I shouted down I would.

.

We landed in Paris early on a Wednesday evening. It was spring and leaves burst like green flame from the sycamores along the wide boulevards. Vendors clustered around small carts, selling exotic sweets and magazines with bright covers and cigarettes. Off on the horizon was the Eiffel Tower, grand and ornate, against billowy gray clouds. Everywhere was bustle, and verve.

My heart swelled with it. Horses drew dark, frocked carts, in them stylishly dressed mademoiselles seated beside men in melon-colored shirts, lovers, amused at antiquity, the cars beeping by them, many of them like Jim Byron's, and all colors. In the Latin Quarter kabobs hung from wires in shop windows; nearly fluorescent candies beckoned. I wanted to try them all.

Our rooms, at a small, fifth rate hotel, were charmingly worn, the beds cavernous and bowed, the floors ancient, warped.

On the Boul' Mich, we sat on a bench, eating croissants. I drank it all in, as if some elixir, in some rapture at the familiar otherness of it.

This was the world my mother had so yearned for.

Yet all of that was just so much irritation for my father. The phones were different, he complained, and hard to use. The food peculiar. The people haughty and cold, he said. And *no one* was on time, which, to him, was the greatest failure.

And, it irritated my father that the police (or should I say a private division of the police), having taken a substantial sum of money for their services, were now asking for more.

They had found my mother, after all, they argued. Not in Germany—but in France. In Paris.

They're having said so, but not delivering her to my father—for legal reasons he was well of aware of—put him in a near rage, and he paced in his room, pounding the adjoining wall to our suite when Bobby and the Twins got to jumping on the beds.

Lisle and Lisa and Bobby were having a grand time, now that they had being reunited with our mother to look forward to, and my father let us out to wander the Latin Quarter with a man he'd hired, someone I suspected he'd paid to forcibly grab my mother and strong-arm her back to the hotel if we caught sight of her.

That I might be some kind of bait almost made me queasy.

So, outside, while the twins and Bobby ate themselves sick on the Quarter candies, I was anxious, and moody, confused over what I should do. And even back in the hotel, while the twins and Bobby watched television, I brooded.

Finally, I locked myself in the bathroom, taking with me a pen and piece of paper. I'd meant to think things out, make lists, like my father did: assets in a column on the left, liabilities on the right.

In the end, I could only think to write a note, just one word on it, which I folded into a tiny square, and put in my pocket.

.

"So, Reenie," my father said, the third afternoon of our waiting. "We'll have this over in no time at all now, won't we."

I felt torn, but steeled myself against him, sitting beside him on that Boul' Mich bench.

I might have gone for that ploy, his promise of a return to our happy family, but hungry just then, I recalled the afternoon we'd left. We'd had nothing to eat, really, and my father had taken those boxes of experimental cereal from the cupboard.

"Just to tide us over," he'd said.

We'd silently filled our bowls and poured on the milk. He'd mixed the boxes all together, so the clots were mixed in with the blobs, which were mixed in with the flakes, and the molasses O's, and so on. It was revolting. But it was those ear-like peach halves that got to me.

I suffered eating my portion by not breathing through my nose.

Bobby said, "Yuck!" and was promptly slapped.

The twins swallowed each mouthful with great dignity, I thought.

"Each box is fortified with vitamins," my father said. "So just think how complete this stuff must be, nutrition-wise, mixed together like this."

"What do you say, Reenie," he said, giving my shoulder a squeeze. "We'll have things ship-shape and in order in no time, won't we.

"It'll all be just like it used to be," he'd said. "Good as new."

On that Boul' Mich bench, sitting miserably beside my father, I held the memory of that last supper in my mind, and did so again, later, crossing the roundabout to the Arc de Triomphe, where we were to meet my mother.

As we made our way to it, cars swerved around us. Men hell-bent over the handlebars of motorcycles honked. A policeman cursed, shouting something about a tunnel, and then we were across. A crowd of tourists stood on one end, gawking, while, opposite, under the cool, dark arch, there stood my mother:

She was wearing a pillbox hat and champagne silk suit, as always, beautiful.

After all my father's talk about how off-the-deep-end she'd gone (her having dumped her art professor *boyfriend* to live in a tiny flat in Paris, he'd said, was *certifiable*) I had expected something more dramatic—a beret pulled low over her forehead, a black leather jacket and handbag, flat-soled shoes. Or some haggard, glassy-eyed, worn-down look. Feverish hallucinations and such.

197

But there she waited, in silk, and her skin rosy, stylish in matching gloves and pearl earrings.

Statuesque. Yet fragile, this Audrey Hepburn-ish something in her.

I could barely breathe, holding Lisle and Lisa, and Bobby, back.

I remember having wanted to hurl myself into her arms, where I would have wept uncontrollably (and, I saw from the quiver in her mouth, she would have too). But I did no such thing. I clung to the twins, gripped Bobby's hand, keeping him at my side.

"Let go," Bobby said, "you're crushing my fingers."

My father strode out and away from us. Broad back, clean, precise stride. A military stride. We knew it well. He stopped feet from my mother. Then they embraced, or should I say, she embraced him, one hand around his neck pulling him closer, the other hand, on his chest, holding him back. They spoke only seconds, I'm sure, but it felt like a lifetime passing there. Then our father craned his head around, and smiling, swung his arm up.

And it was then, I noticed a man among the tourists nod solemnly.

I released the twins and Bobby, who ran crying to her, and I, with my hand in my pocket, forced myself to take smaller, and smaller steps toward her, as if that way we'd have eternity.

.

I recall now the Arc above us suddenly expansive and wide as the sky, that stretch of gray concrete between us, a runway. I took one uncertain, but determined step after another.

I recall, the smell of wool, and a green, wet smell, and exhaust and, passing a woman in a red jacket, the finest rose perfume.

I pinched the back of my hand, then pinched harder, so as not to cry, because I couldn't help it, my eyes were glassing up, my throat burning, yet I knew if I cried, it would all be ruined.

Approaching that happy little circle, I smiled—for my mother—my mouth dry, and lips stretched as if some foreign substance over my teeth.

"Mother," I said, my voice echoing in my head, and she embraced me.

And in that moment, just then, I breathed deeply, one momentous, possessive intaking—smelled: her bath powder, the scent of her hair, her skin, which had the faintest touch of clove and lavender—and pressed into her hand the note I had written in our hotel and stepped back.

.

At the airport we waited behind our gate, watching the clock, my father pacing, at first with irritation, and finally with an ostensible, angry fear. My mother, who had agreed to return home with us there at the Arc, was some forty minutes late now. My father nodded to the detective he'd hired to strong-arm my mother onto the plane, if that became necessary, who marched to a phone.

Moments later he returned. My mother had given the men who'd followed her to her flat the slip, had used a public restroom and gone out the back.

"She used sometheeng to go open the serveece door," he whispered to my father.

I closed my eyes, felt myself falling through an abyss.

"We'll stay here; see what you can do," my father said, and pushed a bill into the detective's hand.

Still, it was hours before we were certain of my mother's desertion of us. I sat morosely with my blue Tourister, pulling at the name tag. I had done something momentous—but was what I'd done... stupid? Selfish? Maybe even—*what?*

Bobby began to cry and I held him until he cried himself out and slept, curled on a chair. Lisle had taken to biting her fingernails, and now she'd gotten them down to the quick. Lisa excused herself to go to the bathroom and returned, her eyes bloodshot and swollen.

Sitting in that uncomfortable plastic chair, loudspeakers paging passengers—my mother included—I tried to make some sense of what I'd done. The old saying, *he cut off his nose to spite his own face* came to me. I wondered if I'd done that.

"We'll just wait a little while longer," my father told an airport official. "I'm sure she's just lost, since she's... sick," he said. "Not right in her mind."

I smiled at that, in some small way, vindicated.

Run, my note had read. Just that.

And hours later, after enormous upheaval, my father causing quite a stir, cursing his detective and the French police and all of France, and Europe along with it, we were put on a flight home.

Over the Atlantic, I sat by the window, the twins asleep across the aisle, Bobby to my left, his head in my lap. My father, in the seat in front of me, was reading a copy of *Scientific American* he'd bought at the airport.

I turned to my right, pressed my face against the cool glass. The moon was out. I watched it ride the wing outside the window.

I imagined my mother, a glass of wine in her hand, similarly bound for who-knew-where, a plane carrying her high above the clouds.

My father turned the page of his magazine, forced it flat against his upraised knee.

I sunk back into my seat and closed my eyes, suddenly barely able to breath.

And as in some old movie, I imagined pins whirled across my map at home; pages of calendars, caught by a spirit wind, tore back, days, weeks, months, and I saw us meeting in some sunny place, a future which, truly, would come to pass.

(And we would see her, back in St. Paul. And know her through those turbulent years of the Sixties, and Seventies, and would love her, in her wild scarves, and crazy shoes, and zany sunglasses, my mother, without exception, the one to visit us—the twins, and Bobby, and myself—and to write cards, and call on the telephone, and send birthday gifts, the gifts always arriving a week early. She would attend our weddings, and the christening of our children; would offer, over the years, summers in exotic places, but not one of us would ever visit her, so adamant was I against it.

When I would, we agreed, we all would.)

But that night, in my imagination, my mother's silver plane with slender wings eased over a dark, rippling ocean, bound for—

I imagined: Tangier. Or was it, St. Petersburg? Or Florence?

At a window seat, bathed in blue light, she lifted her glass, in it champagne, and from somewhere distant, I imagined, Piaf sang, her voice sweet, and bold, yet unutterably sad, *Non, Je Ne Regrette Rien.*

.

And yesterday, I pinned my mother's calendar to my cupboard door, heard that voice again as I stabbed the tack through the glossy paper into the soft pine, so the calendar wouldn't fall—no, no chance of that—so I would see it daily in the coming year, until I relented.

Even knowing then, at my cupboard, I would.

That *some*time, *some*where the moment had already passed, and all that remained for me was to admit it, and I would respond to my mother's spell once again, and fly out to see her.

Acknowledgements

No book makes it into the air without an angel or two under its wings, and *On the Observation Car* had many. I'd like to thank my former Iowa Workshop teachers, Madison Smartt Bell, Jack Leggett, James Alan McPherson, Jane Smiley, and Frank Conroy, who read early drafts of the stories in this collection, for their invaluable insights and observations. Thanks, also, to Louise Erdrich, for citing the title story in *Best American Short Stories*, and to the editors who saw these stories into print. Again, I thank Benn Dunnington, publisher extraordinaire and technician *par excellence*, for his expertise in all things digital, and for carrying on boldly, and with élan, in the face of all odds. A shout out isn't enough, old friend—so here's to that truckload of frogskins at the end of the rainbow. I lift my glass to you! I thank Christina Pellegrino for her truly gorgeous cover artwork. And, always, I thank my lovely wife, for laughing in the funny parts, and for dancing, be it two-step or tango, through all the rest. *Jioia della mia Vita!* I thank every last story angel, of every color, creed, and stripe, for singing in my ear. Don't ever stop, even if it seems I've, temporarily, neglected to listen. One can only sleep so long, to wake once again.

www.ingramcontent.com/pod-product-compliance
Lightning Source LLC
Chambersburg PA
CBHW060926180626
46817CB00004B/1414